The Viridian Rift

Copyright © 2023 Nathan Harms

All rights reserved. No part of this publication may be reproduced or transmitted in any form or by any electronic or mechanical means, including photocopying, recording or by any information storage and retrieval system, without the express written permission of the copyright holder, except where permitted by law. This book is a work of fiction. Any names, characters, places, and incidents are either the product of the author's imagination or, if real, used fictitiously.

Self-Published

Written and Illustrated by Nathan Harms

Visual Edits by Caleb Harms

ISBN: 979-8-8599-7701-7 (paperback)

ISBN: 979-8-8599-7712-3 (hardcover)

Also available on Kindle

~Contents~

Nicolette..1
Madam Duplantier................................15
The Garden...25
At Midnight's Edge..............................35
The Sacrifice..47
An Unpronounceable Name.................57
The Elders..67
Erra...77
Mr. Star..87
The Rift..95
The Great General 103
In War & Sorrow................................113
The Green Sea....................................121
Time & Time Again...........................131

*This work contains modified excerpts from the novel:
Little House in the Big Woods.*

Published 1932. Written by: Laura Ingalls Wilder

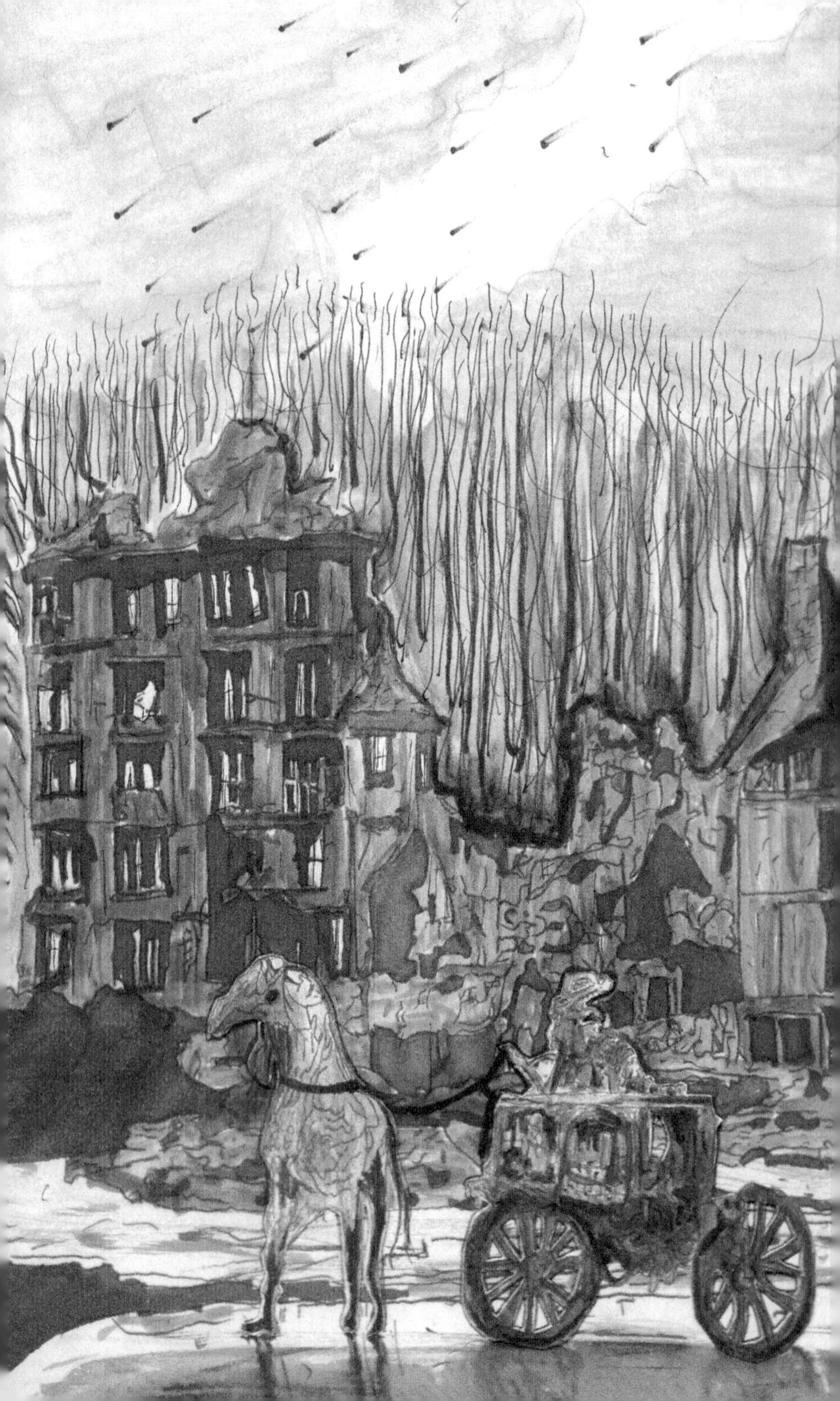

~ Chapter One: Nicolette ~

On darkened nights, thrust upon eager mornings, I waited for my parents to hopefully return home to me. These small hours were loud, almost deafening. And although these nights were shadowed, they were still filled with flashes of flame, igniting just outside these shuttered doors, and cracked windows, illuminating the skies and leaving behind helpless death and murky paths. I was young, in my tenth year. But I was also frightened and alone, forced to act ages beyond that of my own as the entire world fell apart around me. Would my parents return home on this fateful night? Or had they already been swallowed up by a wall of ash and fangs? Suddenly there was a burst of fire and light that was fueled by what sounded like thunderous applause and screaming.

It was horrific outside these doors. A world where an enormous beast soared through the skies consuming us. The living grew silent with grief, for there was fear of being painted with the same colors as the dead. This was a canvas of blood and ash. Deep red, with the lingering scent of copper. But I remembered once, not all that long ago when the world was not so lost. A world where fear of losing the ones you loved was fleeting and rare. Not like this. Not like the hobble and drag of an aging warrior who does not break ice nor draw steel. No, it was once beautiful outside these shuttered doors. The birds sang of joyous seasons and the absence of parents just meant that they were perhaps out to dinner. Those were bright days. Days in which we stood taller than the winged beasts of the sky. Days when hope was just a way of life, not an idea that one could only dream about.

The walls shook with no reprieve or mercy. What was I to do? I curled up behind a dresser that sat in the middle of the living room, gazing over at a photo of my parents that was slowly being consumed by dust from these rattled ceilings. I clutched my knees and put my head down, tucking it as far as I could, so that I could pretend to be anywhere but here. I dared not peek outside these cracking windows. I dared not lay my eyes upon the monster of the sky. This was the moment. With screaming explosions and missing parents, it all became *far* too much, and I gave up. The death of hope and innocence. I had no more to say concerning this world's fear and hatred. So, if violence and loss were all the world had to offer, why should I speak at all? I retreated to my inner voice losing myself within silence until hope or meaning someday returned.

The night was long and filled with screams and rattled walls. I tried to find a moment or two of sleep, but with every temporary drift, I would immediately be awakened by some kind of horror. Be it by shaken ground or deafening terror.

As the sun started to creep out from behind the smoke and the weeping, the light gradually made its way into my space of solace. It poked at me and prodded at my meaning, forcing me to raise my chin and eventually open my eyes. The walls had all but vanished, and I was left in the waking of a nightmare. A home that used to stand proudly, now toppled to the ground. The beast had stolen away the hopeful memories that once adorned my crown. I had lost my dreams that used to flow like water from a gentle spring.

Was this all there was ever going to be? Had the days of laughter fallen deep into the past? They now slept behind drowning eyes and stiff throats that refused to let words blossom.

Suddenly, from beyond the thin walls of smoke, a silhouette shone across the ground. A tall shadow of someone, or something, approaching me. It hobbled and moved back and forth, drawing itself closer to me. I clenched my fists tightly, ready to come face to face with whatever the morning had in store for me. Ready to face this monster. Then from the haze, appeared a man. A man who slowly made his way over the rubble and carried a soft gaze and smile with him. He was dressed very properly, with a light blue tie and a tweed jacket, and he was surprisingly not covered in dust or debris. An impressive feat, considering half the city had just been destroyed, and he was currently trudging through these shattered ruins. His eyes were a deep blue that shimmered through the dust and almost illuminated the room with their beauty.

"Nicolette?!" he yelled.

He knew my name. Surely my parents must have known him. He then noticed me, frozen in fear and adorned by ash and soot that delicately blanketed my pale complexion. His very presence confirmed all the fears that had kept me company throughout that deafening night. My parents were missing and feared dead. This man was known as an *orphan maker*. A man whose job was to deliver the news of death and find new homes for any children left alone by way of tragedy within this war.

The beast had taken back to the sky, flying to mysteriously distant places high up in the heavens. We called it The Red Sea because it appeared as big as an ocean wave, drowning all in its path. Eventually, it would bear the hue of all the blood that it had consumed, leaving behind the dry husks of its victims. With every night, one was unsure of whether it would return to their town. Had it consumed what was required to no longer feast? Would reprieve be found for more than a day? No one knew these answers. Which made the very idea of living in such a large city highly impractical. Especially given the blood-drenched circumstances. So, where was I to hide? Where would I be tucked away, out of the mighty eyes of this winged beast and its ash-covered fangs?

"Are you okay?" the man asked as he helped me to my feet.

I nodded. But my eyes were vacant, and my breath was labored. The man assumed that I was just in shock and would eventually calm down and find meaning within this tragedy. I had to stay strong and bury these feelings. This world did not allow for moments of grief, and I had been told every day since the war had started that there was no time for tears. Our survival depended on maintaining composure. But underneath the surface of my silence, I screamed and sobbed, yelling at the heavens, and cursing the creature that had brought this man here upon this solemn morning.

"My name is Louis. I am... well, let's just say that I'm a friend of your parents. I'll be honest with you, Nicolette, we don't know their whereabouts at the moment, and we can't have you left here to take care of yourself. But I haven't given up hope that they might still be alive. They are fighters, your mom and dad. Do you understand what I'm telling you?"

I nodded again, holding back my tears. My heart both broke and raced all at once.

"I am here to take you to the countryside," said Louis. "To stay with your grandmother. At least until we know what happened to your mom and dad."

I couldn't hold them back anymore, and tears slowly streamed down my face. Where most children of my age would not even consider the loss of their parents as a common possibility, these days, it was a concept that was explained to us from the time that we were quite young. Preparing us for the probable outcome that was due to residing on these front lines. My parents were both warriors within their own right. Scientists that were trying to find a weakness to defeat The Red Sea. But now they had both most likely met a warrior's death. I ran over and picked up the old photo of my parents. Smiles. Would I *ever* see their smiles again? My mind raced. I had never met my grandmother. What if she was unkind or solitary? What if she was insane or did not want this now orphaned child?

Louis slowly walked over to me, taking a soft cloth out of his pocket, and trying to dry my tears.

"There, there, Nicolette. Now you know what we say. No time for tears," he said through a forced smile.

I wondered how many children's tears had been collected with that same soft cloth. A collection of silent grief that lived within Louis's memories.

I quickly packed up a few belongings and followed Louis to where the front door had once stood. He picked me up, carrying me across the rubble, and then sat me down once we had reached the street. I looked around at a city on fire. Infinite strings of smoke laced the skyline in a sight both beautiful and frightening. Bodies lined the streets. Shells of smiles and heartbreak. The remains of people who had once loved, wept, lied, yelled, and laughed. Now nothing more than vacant tombs of flesh and bone. Most of the buildings were toppled and chard. The beast's breath had consumed all that was once beautiful. How would we ever rebuild what once was?

"No time for tears," I whispered to myself.

I stepped into the waiting carriage. It was led by a fifteen-foot-tall creature known as a Kelpie. A strangely shaped horse that was named after old folklore and rumor. Stories from the past had suggested that this strange creature could shapeshift or even take the form of one of us. But the truth was far less exciting. In all reality, they were simply horrifyingly misshapen horses that growled and shrieked with every movement. As if their bones were breaking underneath the weight of each step they took. I peered out the window as we made our way through the city. A city still on fire. A city deep in mourning. This city had not been attacked so violently in several months. As such, bricks and stones had once again been re-stacked. With never knowing where The

Red Sea would strike next, the city had let its guard down and rebuilt, hopeful that the beast would never return. Families once again felt safe. Laughter was once again heard. But no more. No more stones or bricks. No more being safe. No more laughter.

"Do you like art?" Louis asked awkwardly, trying to catch my attention away from all the horror that we were passing by.

I did not reply.

"I love to paint," Louis continued. "In fact, before all this awfulness, I was actually a fairly accomplished artist."

I tried to ignore Louis. Not out of rudeness, but because I was simply at a loss, in shock, and barely aware of what was happening. Looking back, I now know that he was just trying his best to comfort me.

"Perhaps someday, I can teach you how to paint," said Louis, before we returned to silence.

As we approached the outskirts of the city, the smoke began to clear, and the skies once again started to bloom into hues of blue and white, no longer trapped behind veils of shadows and decay. Away from the horrors of death that now clung to the air like breath to lungs. There were wildflowers and creatures that scurried about, untamed, and free to live as they pleased. Strange creatures that had found their way through The Viridian Rift. But unlike The Red Sea, these creatures were not as dangerous as the monster that had chosen to reduce cities to ash.

We traveled well throughout the day, until eventually, the night started to set in. My silence had survived the traveled steps thus far. It was pitch black as we were incredibly far away from any city that might lend its candlelight to our lonely night sky. But the Kelpie's eyes lit the way. Glowing yellow, softly illuminating the dirt road before us. A journey far away from the beast of the sky. Far away from death. Far away from danger. That night, I did not dream, but I did sleep. Exhaustion had overtaken my *every* thought until I was simply a pawn to tired eyes and shallow breaths.

As morning's light finally pierced through the stars, I awoke with a slight stretch and a yawn. There was then a small moment where I had forgotten about why I was there. Why my heart was broken. Why I was sobbing behind these glassy eyes.

"No time for tears," I repeated.

Louis was still fast asleep. I looked out the carriage window, scanning the open and empty fields for anything worth seeing. Then in the distance, I saw it. A house. A giant house. A mansion. One which was surrounded by green trees and gigantic gardens. The kind that someone could surely get lost in. I shook Louis's arm, waking him, and then pointed out the window.

"Ah yes," Louis said with a yawn. "It appears as if we have arrived. I'm sure your grandmother will be *very* relieved to see you. Even if under these unfortunate circumstances."

The carriage made its way up a long trail, passing beyond a giant metal gate, and through tree groves that stood at both sides of the path. Peach trees and cherry blossoms were everywhere. It was gorgeous out here. I reached within my being, trying to find some kind of hope. Perhaps my grandmother would not be so bad. Maybe she would be kind and warm. Maybe she would tuck me in every night and read me stories. My overactive imagination was torturous to my sanity. Maybe my parents would be found soon. I hadn't given up all my strained faith. Not yet. I refused to. And then, once they were found, they could leave the city, and we could all stay here. Why not? We could all make a new life under soft suns and cherry blossoms.

The carriage pulled up to the front of the mansion. I eagerly got out, but my grandmother was not there to greet us. No one was, in fact. It was as if the whole mansion had been abandoned. Louis got out after me and abruptly made his way to the front door. He knocked loudly. Then after a moment or two, locks could be heard on the other side of the door, one after another, being undone. It had to be at least ten different locks, scraping, and turning so that the front door could be opened.

"Very safe," Louis whispered to me with a reassuring wink.

The door slowly opened, revealing an elderly man. He wore a nasty scowl and a patch-covered jacket that looked to be as aged as himself. His beard was scraggly and almost seemed to bounce with every breath that he took. As if it was a struggle to find enough air to keep him alive. His dirty knuckles and stained shirt screamed that he was clearly hired help, as he did not have the swagger of a man who owned a mansion.

"Hello," started Louis. "My name is…"

"I know who you are," interrupted the elderly man.

"Ah yes, I take it that Ms. Duplantier received my message then?" Louis asked.

"Yes… unfortunately," he replied. "Well, come in. Come in."

I followed close behind Louis and the elderly man.

"I take it this is Nicolette?" he asked.

I did not reply. Just silence stacked upon silence.

"She's barely spoken a word since I pulled her from the rubble," Louis said.

"Hmmm," said the elderly man. "Well, that won't do. You'll have to speak up around here if you want to be taken care of. We're not mind readers. You understand?"

"Yes sir," I mumbled.

"And what is your name?" asked Louis.

"I'm Oswald. Head of property upkeep and assistant to anything and everything that Madam Duplantier demands or requires," Oswald replied with an obvious sense of pride.

Oswald led Louis and I down a long hall. Eventually, we arrived at an incredibly small room. A room roughly the size of a closet, which was equipped with a simple dresser, nightstand, and a sparse bed. No bright colors, no toys, no books. Nothing that would imply that this room was meant to house a child.

"This is where you'll sleep. Breakfast is at first light, lunch will be promptly at noon, and supper shall be served at 6:00 pm on the dot," said Oswald.

"Ah yes," started Louis. "And what should she do in her free time? You know, for fun?"

Oswald looked noticeably disgusted by Louis's question.

"Fun?!" scoffed Oswald.

"Yes, fun," said Louis. "After all, she *is* a child."

"Very well. In her free time, she may reside in her room, in the library, or outside."

Oswald looked at me, proceeding to lean in until he was mere inches from my face. He carried a grimace, and I could smell the revolting scent of tobacco dripping from him.

"But I must warn you, Nicolette. Do not go into the garden! Do not even think about it! It is off limits!" Oswald yelled.

Louis was quite surprised by the tone that had erupted from Oswald. His anger had appeared out of nowhere, inappropriately elevated for deeds that had yet to be committed.

"I'm sure she will be on her best behavior, Mr. Oswald," Louis interjected, attempting to calm Oswald down. "Isn't that right, Nicolette?"

I nodded slowly and carefully. Why was this elderly man yelling at me? I just wanted to be cared for. I was never one to cause much trouble and had seldom done anything that could be construed as rebellious.

"Let us hope so," Oswald said.

"I was hoping to speak to Ms. Duplantier before I headed back to the city," said Louis.

"Madam Duplantier is busy I'm afraid. So that will not be possible. Say your goodbyes to the child," instructed Oswald.

Louis was reluctant to leave me under the supervision of a caretaker and a phantom. But he had no choice. There was much to be done back in the city. He had to find out what had happened to my parents, and also try and find new homes for several more children. He crouched down and smiled at me.

"Alright then, your grandmother and Mr. Oswald will take exceptionally good care of you. I'll return once I've discovered what happened to your mother and father. Okay?"

I nodded in hesitant agreement. I hoped that this would not be the last I'd see of Louis.

"I'll let you get settled," Oswald snarled at me.

They both left me alone in that closet-sized room. I climbed up on the bed. I could feel springs poking through the mattress and it made an awful screech with every movement that I took. How was I supposed to sleep here? I peered out the window, watching Louis's carriage leave, down the long path, and passed the metal gate until eventually, he faded out of my sight. I was now left alone, a stranger in a strange house. A future uncertain, and a past both tragic and silent.

"No time for tears," I said softly.

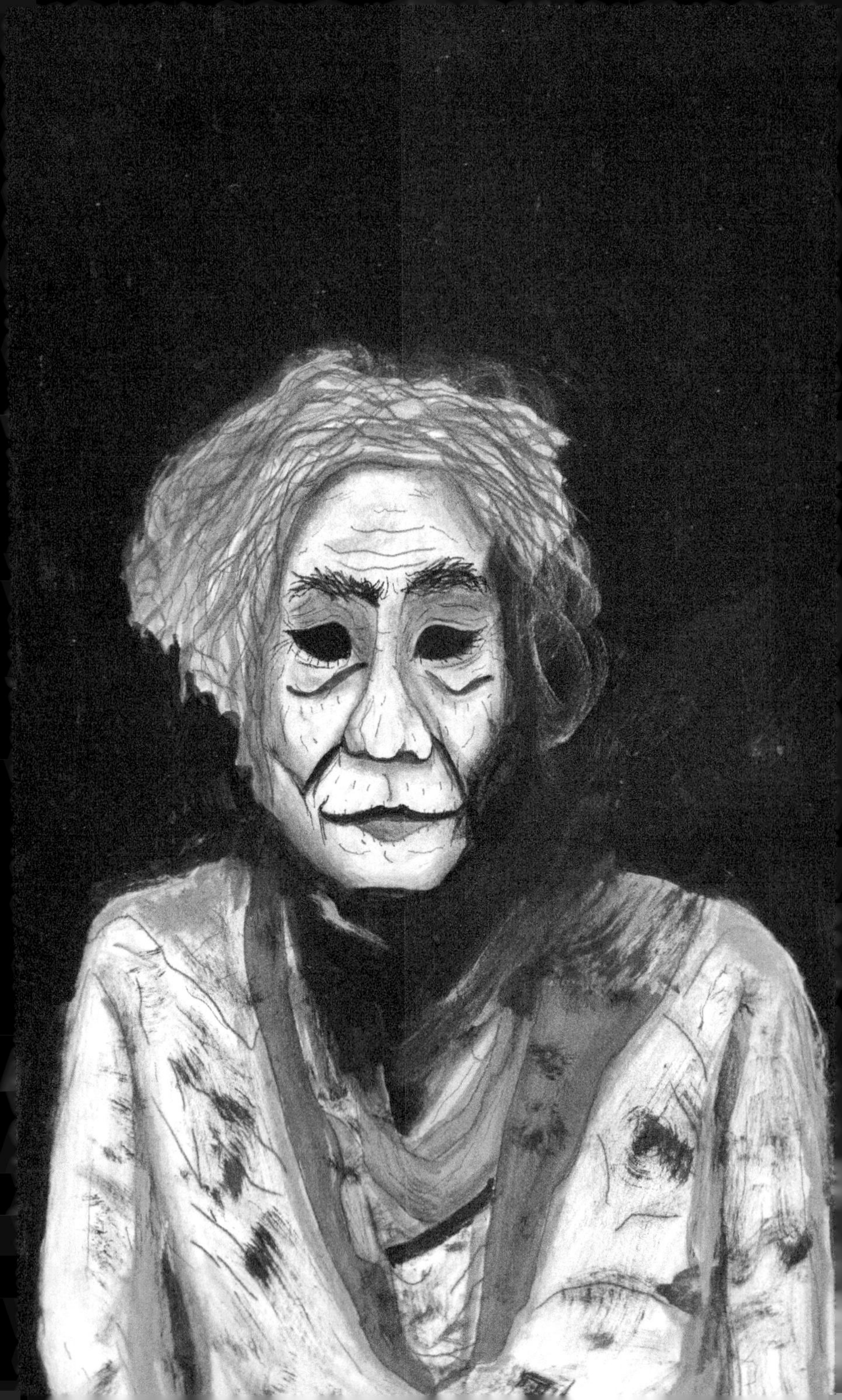

~ Chapter Two: Madam Duplantier ~

Eyes open. I was jolted awake by the echoed sounds of screaming and fire, accompanied by thunder and death. These sounds had seeped into my dreams and poisoned my mind with memories of The Red Sea and its blinding fury. I could not sleep soundly in this mysterious and cold house. A mansion of secrets and random clatters that disrupted any hope for a peaceful night's rest. All I had seen of it, thus far, was my closet-sized room. Even dinner was spent within these walls, as Mr. Oswald had brought me my supper earlier in the night, leaving it at my door. Steamed vegetables and pot roast. It was almost within the realm of being delicious. Well, at the very least, it was edible. Or maybe I was just *so* hungry that I had been incredibly forgiving when it came to the vegetables being soggy, and the pot roast being bland. But even with a full belly and a roof above my head, I could not sleep soundly, and the night begged me to explore it.

I looked over at the sparse nightstand. The only thing that it held was the faded photograph of my parents that I had rescued from dust and ashes. Happier days. I couldn't help but imagine their screams and horror as The Red Sea devoured them… as if I were there to witness it. When embraced by tragedy, it is hard not to imagine the last moments of those whom you love. It was too much. It was awful. But I could not stop thinking about their last thoughts. Were they about me? Were they worried about what would happen to me if they did not survive? I had to shake these thoughts loose from my obsession. Without thinking I jumped to my toes, feeling the cold wooden floor beneath my steps. I missed the wool socks that I would wear in the mornings. They had always felt warm against my step and made even the most chilled floors feel inviting. I pulled open the door and inched down the darkened hallway. Cautious. Careful to not make a sound.

Framed images lined the walls. Paintings I hadn't noticed upon my arrival. They held the images of flowers and trees with clouded horizons tucked behind them. Not the most competent paintings I had ever seen, but their colors were oddly soothing. Just shades upon shades of green, almost shimmering and moving like a soft ocean entangled by a cool breeze. As if they longed to hypnotize my tired eyes and lull me back to sleep. I left the darkened hall behind, finding myself in the foyer, looking upon tiled floors that rose to soaring ceilings and held web-incrusted chandeliers. Dust caked every inch of everything. Surely Mr. Oswald was far too elderly to reach each darkened corner of this massive chateau. But there seemed to be no other staff around. At least none that I had seen thus far. Which seemed highly impractical, given the size of such a property.

It was eerily quiet. Only the occasional rattle could be heard. A slight gust of wind or a subtle knock upon the walls. But these sounds did not frighten me. No, I was used to the murmurs brought forth by old houses. It was a natural occurrence. Like lightning, or rain. I looked to my right. There was a large door. From beneath its presence, I could see a warm light. Its orange hue looked to be from a fireplace. My curiosity gripped me, dragging me towards the door, and inviting me inside. I slowly opened it.

The walls were lined with books from floor to ceiling. Mr. Oswald had made mention of a library, and it was one of the few places I was told I was allowed to venture under these restricted ceilings. From epic tales of romance to horrifying stories that featured the undead, and every kind of book in between. They were all here, scattered amongst these walls. Even books that one might not expect to find in the other's company, such as books filled with fairytales cradled next to books on religion. Although I guess it would be fair to say that these two genres did seem to switch places with one another every few lifetimes. Yes, anything you could ever desire to know somehow lived upon these shelves. I could practically hear all the books breathe as their pages longed to be touched and read. They called to me and my ever-curious imagination.

"You must be my granddaughter," said an unseen voice.

I was startled. I had been so perplexed by the books before my eyes that I had forgotten to look around and observe anyone's presence besides that of my own. I slowly walked over to the giant black leather chair that sat directly in front of a massive fireplace. Sitting there, with a book in her lap and a stale expression across her face, was my grandmother, Ms. Duplantier. She did not smile. She did not even look like she was capable of such a thing. She wore fine linens and a soft scowl. Her hair was unkempt, and her skin was wrinkled like wet leather. I was quiet at first. I still had a strange desire to hold my voice hostage. I could remember the walls falling all around me. I could remember the heartbreak that had draped itself across my lonely existence within the midst of fires and loss, killing my innocence. And as such, I still lacked words, for fear that I might just cry.

"I heard that you were barely speaking?"

"Yes, ma'am," I whispered.

"Probably for the best. I do like things quiet around here."

Her voice was gruff. As if *every* word she spoke was a chance to scold whomever had volunteered their time to listen. She did not look at me. She just stared deeply into the fire as if captivated by its very existence. Was I in trouble? Was she angry at me? I approached her and sat on the ground next to her mighty shadow. The room then grew silent for an awfully long time. The only sound in the air was the crackle of the fire and the occasional gust of wind knocking against the walls from outside. Then finally, breaking the silence, my grandmother began to speak again.

"Your mother was a most troublesome child. Bet she didn't tell you that. Did she?" she asked.

I replied with a shake of my head, even though I was sure she didn't see it as she had not even bothered to look in my general direction for a single second.

"She would run all around the property, playing outside every day until the setting of the sun. Digging in the dirt, playing in the garden. Laughing, screaming, tracking mud all throughout the house."

She at last turned and looked at me. A slight grin attempted to reveal itself for the briefest of moments.

"You look like your mother," she said.

I smiled. It was the first time I had smiled since I had woken surrounded by rubble and smoke. My mother's beauty was something that no one in their right mind could ever possibly deny. To be compared to those dark blue eyes and perfect smile would be a compliment to anyone. I couldn't stop thinking about her now. My thoughts finding their way to the likely truth that I would never see her again. The most obvious of thoughts from someone newly consumed by grief. A catastrophic idea. One that I did not intend to feed with my growing concern. My smile faded as my grandmother's eyes once again looked at the flames.

"As you know, dark days are upon us. My time is almost up, so I shall not have to carry this burden for much longer. But you. You may live long enough to see how all of this concludes."

She was of course referring to the savage war that was being waged across the world. All of us fighting against The Red Sea. A singular demon from above, that seemed to have no weakness. When The Viridian rift had first crept open, beautiful colors poured into our world. Fogs and rains that were laced in various shades of green. Initially, we thought it was the entrance to some kind of afterlife. But we quickly realized that it was a doorway to a mysterious world. And when there are doorways, someone is bound to cross their threshold. Would it be us, or them? It turns out it was them.

At first, all that arrived were simple little creatures. Strange, small, and beautiful. They materialized out of the green fog that made its way through the rift, setting them down across our lands, and releasing them into our world. But they were nothing to haunt nightmares. Then bigger creatures began to arrive. True, they were strange, and some were even frightening. But none seemed particularly violent, at least towards humans. However ultimately, The Red Sea arrived. One day it ripped through the rift and began to devour all in its path. Pulling the blood from all it touched. As tall as a building, with the voice of a storm. It thundered throughout our lands, leaving nothing but death and devastation in its path. It was hard to decipher if it was even alive, or if it was just another world's enraged storm, turning ours into a tomb.

I cleared my throat, considering speaking. But what would I even say? What could a child, such as I, bring to this subtle silence? I glanced around the room. Aside from the rows and rows of books, there were more framed paintings. Clearly created by the same mind as the ones I had seen in the hall. Beautiful, almost hypnotic, shades of green that seemed to float off the canvas, accompanied by fairly generic shapes of flowers, bushes, and trees. I couldn't take my eyes off them. Which was something my grandmother then seemed to notice.

"It's the colors that you see first. Isn't it?" she asked me.

Even though I was enamored with the paintings, I managed to nod my head, almost in a trance as I stared deeply into their presence. The colors practically glowed while whispering at me to come closer.

"I'm not much of an artist. But after the rift opened, Mr. Oswald, in his kindness, went and fetched me an assortment of the green hues that had fallen from that other world. Their various shades made my paintings... well... *almost breathe*. As if bringing them to life. Now I've filled many of the walls in this empty mansion with these strange, glowing peeks at the other side. It is an eccentric obsession."

She had Mr. Oswald fetch her these colors? But how? The rift that had opened was thousands of miles away from here, somewhere near the frozen forest. It had taken many months for the various creatures and The Red Sea to migrate this far after the rift had appeared. It took almost just as long for the tales of its existence to spread. This was, of course, a few years ago. Now, a portal in the sky, over the frozen forest, which spewed life from another world, had become common knowledge to everyone.

"I will assume that Mr. Oswald has informed you of the house rules," she chuckled. "He is one for the theatrics. However, I must insist that no matter what you do, you do not, under *any* circumstances, enter my garden."

Her tone was abruptly serious. As if our very survival depended on me not crossing the garden's gate and peering inside. Naturally, after being told this by multiple people, I could now only think of my desire to break this rule. As children, when told what we can and cannot do, it is quite common for us to want to do the opposite. One would think that at my grandmother's age, she would share in the knowledge and not make such a big deal out of an important rule.

"Do you understand?" she asked me.

I nodded, reassuring her. Again, not sure if she could even see me, as her eyes were still drawn to the flames.

"Well, pick out a book for the night and go read it until your eyes grow heavy," she instructed. "In the morning, you can explore the house."

I slowly got up and proceeded to look through all of the literary offerings that were present. Then a book caught my eye. *Little Cottage in the Wilderness.* A story that my mother had read to me before. About a little girl named Laura and her life growing up in the woods of a strange and distant land. A story about both hard work and fun. I smiled. I could hear my mother's voice ring throughout my thoughts.

"She thought to herself, 'This is right now.' She was happy that the little cottage, and her ma and pa, and the warm fire, and the music, were right now. They could not be forgotten, she thought, because now is now. It can never really be a long time ago."

This was my favorite part. At the time it seemed so hopeful. But now that my mother was most likely gone, it seemed... incredibly sad. A single tear crawled down my cheek, splashing upon the book and its worn cover. I clutched the book in my arms and started to head back towards my room while reminding myself that there was no time for tears.

"Goodnight, Nicolette," my grandmother said, just as I had reached the door. "I hope you enjoy your book and sleep well."

I quickly made my way back to that closet-sized room. Once there, I curled up into a little ball atop my uncomfortable mattress and held the book that I had borrowed tightly. I held it like it was my mother. A small piece of my history. A reminder of what was once now but was now then. Cradled in my arms like it was the only thing tethering me to her love and breath. And then I slept. Consumed by memories of the past, and a spirited demeanor for the sunrise. For at first light, I would go exploring.

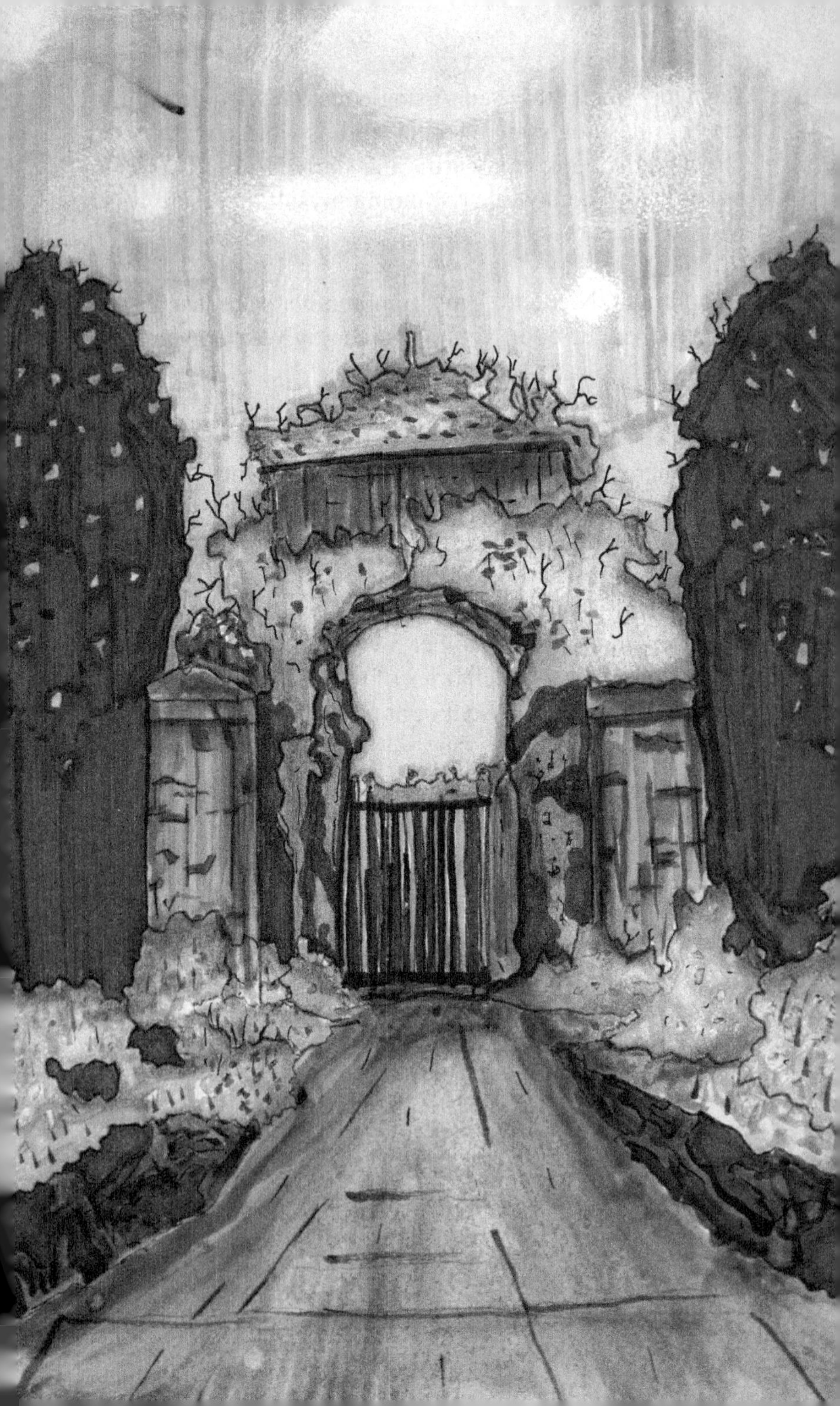

~ Chapter Three: The Garden ~

I was slow to wake up that next morning. I had tossed and turned the night away. On occasion, I had found myself being jabbed by the book that I had cradled throughout my empty sleep. As my eyes squinted with the rising sun, I thought about the sound of birds. One of the *very* few things that I remembered from life before the rift. Now the birds all remained silent. Predatory rat-like creatures, which had been nicknamed The Blind Venom, had almost completely wiped out the entire population of morning birds. Those that remained had adapted to not alert these strange creatures to their presence. The Blind Venom only came out at night, sticking to the shadows until first light, and doing their best not to interact with humans. As such, no one really knew exactly what they looked like. Only that they were incredibly fast and vicious when it came to all manner of morning birds.

I could smell something wafting down the hall. It smelled like bacon and eggs. It was first light. I needed to hurry if I wanted to get breakfast. I got dressed and ran down the hall, towards the smell of food. My heels chattered against the wooden floors, sending a galloping click reverberating throughout the house. The clicks bounced off the soaring ceilings, eventually dulling themselves out to silence. As I ran into the kitchen, I came face to face with Mr. Oswald's furious scowl. He did not say a word, but his angry eyes stopped me in my place, calming my step, and sending me directly to a chair where I could enjoy breakfast properly and in silence. As Mr. Oswald made my plate, I couldn't help but peer around the room looking for my grandmother.

She was a mystery, but my late-night chat had endured her to me in a rather strange way. She was gruff. But locked behind her rough demeanor, lived a kind heart. She reminded me of my mother. Just certain mannerisms and expressions, sly smiles, and gentle eyes. It was comforting, and I could tell that the fears I had assumed about her were perhaps untrue.

"Looking for Madam Duplantier, I take it?" he asked with a little bit of an annoyed grumble.

I nodded eagerly. I was quite excited to see her.

"Madam Duplantier does not have breakfast. She stays up late and sleeps until almost noon most days. So, I implore you to be quiet while she rests!"

There was an angry nature that erupted from Mr. Oswald. He always assumed that I was going to be a problem, expecting the worst with every passing moment. He had some sort of strange pride in playing the role of my grandmother's imaginary protector, even though I was quite confident that she would be just fine without Mr. Oswald at her side.

"After breakfast, you can go play outside."

"But…" I let a little squeak of my voice escape.

"What was that? Out with it! I thought you weren't talking," he replied with a bit of laughter, mocking me and my choice to barely speak.

I wanted to explore the house, not play outside. But I did not want to discuss it with Mr. Oswald or argue with him on the subject. He was not going to change his mind on what I was, or was not, allowed to do. I would have to assume that this would be my daily routine from now until I was old enough to do otherwise. And so, I remained silent.

"That's what I thought," he said with a bit of a nefarious smirk.

I finished my breakfast of two slices of burnt bacon, one slightly runny egg, and a dry biscuit. Obviously, Mr. Oswald's talents did not appear to include preparing meals. After eating, I turned my attention to playing outside. I would much rather explore the mansion and its many rooms, but Mr. Oswald had made it clear what he was allowing me to do. At least until my grandmother was awake.

The grounds were quite well kept. And as I walked around, exploring, I finally saw other people on the property. Just like I had assumed, there was simply no way the elderly Mr. Oswald could ever care for this much land by himself. There were at least four or five people who were keeping busy pruning bushes and trimming trees.

I wandered around for a long while, breathing in the sweet scent of cherry blossoms and other assorted plants. A soft grin found its way across my mouth. The feeling of being a child, exploring and playing outside. No death around, only soft country air to keep me company. I then found a giant mound of mud and tried to climb to the top of it, sliding and falling on various occasions. I laughed loudly at the hilarity of my stumbled steps. I kept trying to climb the giant mound, eventually making my way to its peak. I was filthy, covered head to toe with mud. But it was worth it, for I had conquered this mountain of dirt like a brave explorer.

One of the caretakers walked over to me and laughed. She was a young woman. Most likely in her late twenties. Her eyes were kind, and her hair was short. She looked as if she had spent much of her own youth climbing hills of mud and making a mess of things.

"Oswald is going to lose his mind if you track any of that in the house!" she yelled.

I shrugged my shoulders and then slid down the mound, immediately standing up proudly and proceeding to try and brush my dress off.

"You must be Nicolette," she said with a smile.

I nodded and smiled back.

"I'm Elisa."

I held out my hand. My father had always taught me that a firm handshake was the best way to make a marvelous first impression. Elisa grabbed my hand and shook it, not caring about the mud that was now passing from my palm to hers.

"Oh my! That, right there, is a *very* firm handshake you have, Nicolette."

I couldn't help but laugh.

"Let's go get you cleaned off," she said.

She led me to her cabin that resided on the grounds. It was fairly small but quite nice inside. Much nicer than any staffing quarters I had ever seen before. She drew me a bath in the washroom and laid out some clean clothes. A dark blue dress that fit me perfectly. Which was both lucky and rather odd. After cleaning myself off and changing, I sat down in Elisa's little living room. She had made some tea and biscuits. The tea's aroma was soft and sweet, and the biscuits were delicious. They reminded me of the ones my mother used to bake. After a few moments of sitting in silence, I cleared my throat. I had not said more than a handful of words since arriving here, but Elisa's generosity prompted me to speak.

"Thank you for the dress. It's beautiful. Where did you get it from?" I asked softly.

Elisa smiled. But not a normal smile. A smile that was laced with sadness and grief. Her eyes practically turned to glass as she tried to force the words out.

"They… um… they belonged to my daughter. She was around your age when… when The Red Sea arrived."

It was a story that I knew all too well. Loved ones lost to the grasp of a monster. Everyone had lost someone. No one was without pain and grief.

"I'm sorry," I whispered.

Elisa did not acknowledge my apology. She just sat there, staring into nothing, deep in thought.

"After… everything had happened. After the rift. After The Red Sea. After… losing my daughter. I ran. I ran as far away from the city as I could. Until, almost dead, starving, and without shelter, I found my way here, and Ms. Duplantier took me in. That's how all of us came to live here. The other hired help and I. We were all lost and grieving, and were somehow, inexplicably, drawn here."

Elisa wiped the tears from her eyes and shivered as if being brought back to reality. The here and now is where she currently lived. Not the breaths of yesterday.

"But enough about all that. I will clean your clothes. It is almost lunchtime for you so you better head back inside."

My stomach turned to think of what Mr. Oswald was going to make for lunch. I had already filled myself up with delicious biscuits. Perhaps I would skip lunch today. I stood to my feet and proceeded to walk to the cabin's front door. I looked out at the massive grounds that covered the property; my eyes immediately drawn to the mysterious garden that I was told I could not enter under any circumstance. I turned back around towards Elisa.

"What's in the garden?" I asked.

Elisa immediately stopped cleaning up the tea and biscuits and looked at me fiercely.

"I don't know, Nicolette. But we aren't supposed to ask about that. I probably shouldn't even be telling you this, but your grandmother is the only one who enters there."

"When?"

"In the dead of night, when she thinks that no curious eyes are watching."

"She's never said why no one else is allowed inside?" I asked.

Elisa shook her head slowly.

"No, child. But when one is given a second chance, shelter, and food, you don't question the only rule that you are given."

She took a deep breath and forced a smile through her obvious discomfort.

"Now, enough about the garden. Off with you. Go have your lunch," Elisa instructed.

I thanked her again for her kindness and the soft blue dress that she had let me borrow. I promised not to get it dirty and swiftly made my way back to the mansion.

Once inside, I was pleased to see my grandmother up and about. Mr. Oswald barely noticed that I had come back inside, as he was busy washing dishes slower than one would think possible. For lunch, we had cucumber sandwiches. I assumed my grandmother had made them herself, as they tasted quite delicious. Even with a stomach full of biscuits, I ate a whole plate of the refreshing little sandwiches. My grandmother kept glancing over at my dress, eventually noticing the mud that was still caked on my shoes. She smirked.

"I take it that you've met Elisa?" she asked.

"Yes," I said softly, unsure if I was about to be in trouble.

"Sad story, that one. Poor girl lost everything. But…we are glad to have her around to…" she chuckled. "…clean up messes."

An unspoken moment where my grandmother knew *exactly* the kind of trouble I had been getting into. She finished her sandwich and her tea and proceeded to stand up.

"Have you been having fun exploring the grounds?" she asked.

"Yes, ma'am," I replied.

"Well, I suggest you spend your afternoon exploring the house," she said with a little wink.

Mr. Oswald grumbled something under his breath before clearing the table and returning to the kitchen.

"Ignore Mr. Oswald. He can be quite grouchy when it comes to maintaining the cleanliness and structure of the house. Go have some fun."

She left the room and disappeared into the library, shutting the door behind her. I wondered if all she ever did was sleep, eat, read, and visit her mysterious garden. But I did not dwell on these questions for long, as there was a house that was begging me to explore it.

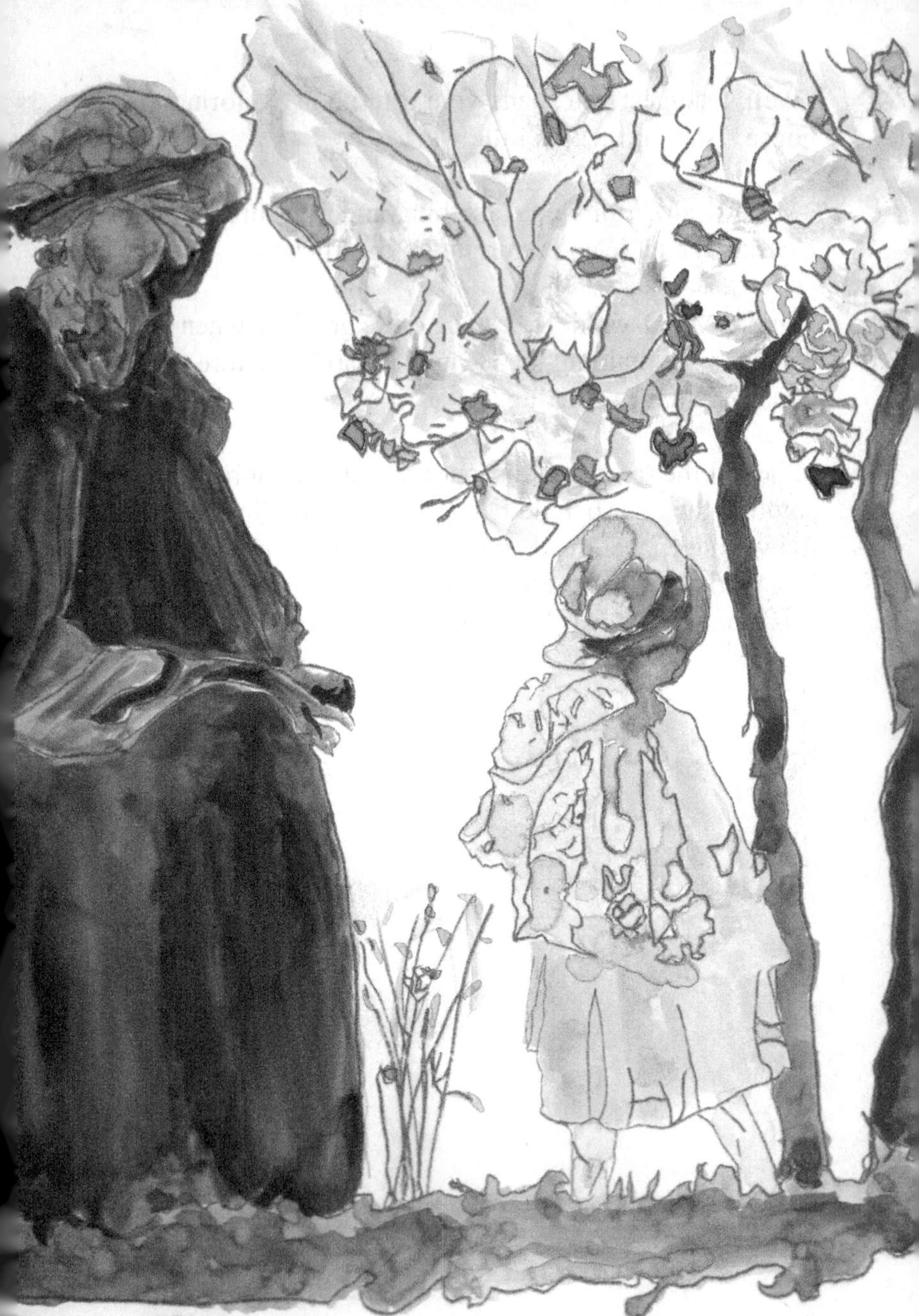

~ Chapter Four: At Midnight's Edge ~

When one is first setting off on mysterious explorations of large mansions, it can be quite daunting. The rooms seem endless and the space eternal. But after several hours, I found myself feeling extremely disappointed at what I had, or rather, had *not* found. Mainly just empty rooms. No beds dwelled within. No family secrets. Just dusty, cold, empty rooms. Rooms that had not had their blinds opened in many years. Stepping into them left footprints upon their dust-covered bones, like walking through snow. A sure sign that no one but I, had opened these doors in an exceptionally long time. I did find a couple of dolls tucked away in a chest. I assumed that they used to be my mother's. I also found a few candles, a purple rug, and some paintings of dogs, clowns, and trains. I imagined that these weathered paintings had once hung on the walls of my mother's room when she was my age.

I gathered these things, my treasures, and slowly made many trips back and forth between these dusty rooms and my closet-sized occupancy. I did not question why I had not been given one of these other rooms. The grounds were endless, and I would rarely be in there anyway. Besides, I would take these random prizes and make this tiny room my own. A refuge from the world and its cold grip.

Mr. Oswald begrudgingly helped me hang the paintings that I had found. I could tell it brought him no joy to hammer nails into these barren walls. With every swing of the hammer, he would mumble soft obscenities under his breath.

Just after sprucing up my dwellings, it was time for dinner. I joined my grandmother in the dining room for roast duck and stuffing. The duck was overcooked, and the stuffing was mushy. Not slightly burnt, how it is supposed to be. But it was still okay, and I could not hold any ill will against Mr. Oswald's culinary prowess. After all, he had spent much of his afternoon helping me hang paintings and move various treasures.

"Mr. Oswald tells me that you found some of your mother's things while exploring the house?" my grandmother asked.

"Yes, ma'am," I replied.

"And he has also told me that you claimed them all for yourself and redecorated your room, putting holes in the walls and cluttering the floors. Is that also true?"

I could not tell what my grandmother was thinking. She did not smile or look at me while she asked these questions. She was simply stoic and cold with her words. But that was just how she talked, and I was slowly learning that her words could not be taken too seriously when first spoken.

"Yes, ma'am. Is that okay?"

My grandmother looked up from her dinner and smiled at me. I breathed a sigh of relief.

"You know, your mother still wanders these halls. Well, at least her memory does. Every creak of the floorboard sings of her step. Every dust-covered room and shut door still echoes with her laughter. I've kept this house locked away because it reminded me of her, and … the relationship that we could have had."

I could see my grandmother get lost in sadness. She had not approved of my mother marrying my father. He was a commoner and my mother had come from great wealth. As such, my grandmother had stopped talking to my mother many years ago, before I was born. It was a choice that my grandmother had made. One that I could tell she regretted with every breath and passing second. A choice that had kept me out of her life, until after my parents had been lost to The Red Sea. So many years and memories vanished to the ticking clocks of time and remorse. My grandmother shook off her sadness and once again smiled at me.

"So, by all means, whatever is needed to make you feel like this is your new home… Whatever treasures you find. It's all yours for the taking."

My grandmother swiftly finished her dinner, without speaking another word, and then made her way back to the library. Mr. Oswald had built her a fire for the night, and she had a worn book waiting for her. I followed close behind, wanting to simply exist in her shadow. To read beside her, and hopefully continue to gain her admiration. The flames from the fire gently reflected across the small headdress that my grandmother wore. It was beautiful. Three white feathers and a soft blue jewel that held her rather unkempt hair in place.

"I like your headdress," I finally said softly.

"Do you?" my grandmother laughed. "It's called an aigrette. It has feathers from an egret and a pretty little blue jewel. Your mother actually made this for me.... Before... Well, before you were born."

I smiled, imagining my mother putting together such a beautiful trinket. I was reminded of all the clothing that she would tailor and make just for me when she was alive. When she was alive? That sounded awful. No. She was *still* alive. They both were. I had to maintain that hope. I had to believe.

We did not speak a word over the next several hours. We just read our books in silence. On occasion, my grandmother would sigh or giggle softly. I had no idea what words were causing such a reaction, but I wanted to experience the same. So, when she would giggle, so would I. When she would sigh, I would mirror her breath. Of course, my book never matched hers and I was quite positive that she saw through my ruse. But without warm arms to cradle me and sing me to sleep, this was the only connection that I could find.

The pages began to blur, and the words started to wander. Eventually, I fell asleep on the ground, using my book as a pillow, and the warmth of the fire as a blanket for my dreaming. The next thing I knew, I felt a soft kiss on my forehead and felt my grandmother take her aigrette and gently place it in my hair. Then I heard the creaking of floorboards. I couldn't help but be drawn out of my sleep. The room was clouded as my head was still stitched to whatever strange dream I was just having. But with what I could make out, I saw my grandmother leave the library, and turn, not towards her room, but towards the back door. I heard it creak open, the gentle wind nipping at the strange paintings that covered the walls, causing them to sway back and forth and sing a haunting melody. But that song was cut short as the door shut behind her, once again leaving the house in silence.

I tried to fall back asleep or work up the strength to make my way to my newly redecorated bedroom, but something else held me like a whisper. Curiosity. Where had my grandmother gone? Was she visiting her garden at this time of night? My inquisitive thoughts became too much to carry, and I found my eyes now wide open, awake, and ready to follow whatever course I was destined to take.

I jumped to my feet and made my way from the library, down the darkened hall, and out the back door. I was quiet within my step, so as not to draw attention to myself. I crept behind my grandmother as she slowly made her way to the garden and its metal gates. Step by step, one foot in front of the other. She stopped at the gate and pulled out an aged key, inserting it in the lock and slowly opening the gate, making her way inside. As it started to close behind her, my curiosity drove my step and forced me to move in haste. I ran towards the gate and just barely made it inside the garden before I was left outside of its mysterious walls. I tried to catch my breath for a moment. But no sooner had I found my stance, I turned and came face to face with my grandmother. She glared at me in silence before speaking a word.

"What in the world are you doing following me in here?!" she yelled.

I was speechless. I did not know what to tell her to make myself look innocent. She had strictly forbidden me from crossing beyond these walls, yet here I stood.

"I'm sleepwalking!" I blurted out.

My grandmother just scowled at me. She was no fool, and my lie was not worth the breath that I had just wasted on it.

"I...I was curious," I finally admitted.

"I told you to never come in here!"

"I know. I'm sorry."

My grandmother was silent for a few more moments. She was thinking. But of what, I did not know. After a minute or two of her placing pieces together within her thoughts, she finally addressed me and my decided fate.

"You really are *just* like your mother. Never listening. Always causing trouble. But, since you are here, and you are my only living relative...I might as well show you."

She quickly turned her back to me and proceeded to venture deeper into the garden's shadowed embrace. I was nervous and immediately regretted following her beyond the library and its warmth.

"Follow me!" she yelled. "We must move quickly, child!"

I tried my best to keep up with her. Even at her age, my grandmother marched through the garden like she was on a mission from God and every second that passed was one too many. As we walked, I began to notice my surroundings. Something that I had forgotten to do earlier. One does not normally remember such details while being scolded. The garden glowed. These were not like the cherry blossoms that gripped the air outside of these walls. These were not roses nor tulips, but other strange flowers and plants. The likes of which I had never seen before. They looked like they had been ripped through the rift and laid to rest upon the soil of this garden.

We walked for an exceedingly long time. After a while, it became clear that the space within this garden was far bigger than it appeared from outside of these walls. As if time and space had been stretched and skewed once the threshold to this place had been crossed. I was unsure as to where we were going. But before I had worked up the courage to ask, we arrived at our destination.

It was a magnificent tree. Taller than any tree I had ever seen before. It glowed green and pulsed slowly, releasing a soft hum into the air as if it were singing a song that had been rendered incomplete or lacking. My grandmother made her way over to it and touched its bark, staining her hands with the various hues of green that seeped off of this strange tree.

I approached the tree. In awe of its presence. It hypnotized me, just like the paintings that hung from the mansion's walls.

"What is this?" I asked.

I was far too young to understand the complexities of everything and all. But I did know that something was strange about small gardens with cities worth of bizarre plants that resided inside of them.

"You know of the one rift near the frozen forest?" she asked.

I nodded. Of course I did. Everyone did.

"Well, what if I told you that there was a second rift? A rift that appeared several months after the first, right here in this garden. Behind these walls. Shifting and stretching reality as we know it. Spilling into this garden and merging our two worlds into one visceral reaction of colors and creatures."

I did not know what to say. I was not sure how to react, and I only had questions.

"Does anyone else know that this is here?" I asked.

My grandmother grew quiet and slowly made her way over to a small moss-covered log so that she might sit down and rest.

"Only Mr. Oswald knows. He was the one who first ventured inside, collecting plants for me to examine. I fell in love with the colors. They…awoke me."

Little flashes of light started to take to the air, far off into the sky, against the backdrop of the star-filled night. But the sky looked strange. There was a haze to it that I had not seen before. As if I was looking at its beauty through stained glass windows.

"I dared not to tell anyone about this rift, for I did not want my house and my colors to be taken away from me. I did not desire to have armies upon my doorstep."

"Why do you come here at night?" I asked.

"To look to the sky, Nicolette. To view its beauty. And to talk to the colors. I get lost in here for hours at a time, every single night."

I was not sure if it was selfish or beautiful for my grandmother to keep this place to herself. The world was dying and yet my grandmother was the guardian of the biggest secret that had ever been.

"Have you seen the second rift? How far from here is it? What does it look like?" I asked.

"It is many miles from here, yet still within these very walls. And yes, I have seen it one time, when it first opened, and that other world began spilling out into the garden. It took a full day to travel there. It's a giant gateway of revolving colors and clouds that sits on the ground like a doorway. A door in which a foolish person could walk right through."

"You mean you could touch it?!" I exclaimed.

"If I were a foolish person, yes."

The other rift was located far up in the sky. Far too high for anyone to ever reach it. If the world only knew that another rift existed, one that could be entered, then they would have all descended upon this garden like waves in a storm. Anything to stop The Red Sea. I almost understood why my grandmother had been so secretive about this place. But then I thought about my parents. They had sacrificed everything for this war. As scientists, I remembered them always talking about how much easier it would be to gain the upper hand if they could simply get close enough to study the rift. So, all this death, and pain, and horror. But this whole time, my own grandmother had perhaps held the key to winning this war.

As soon as I had thought this, the plants began to glow red, and a buzzing sound started to reverberate through the garden. It was incredibly loud, almost deafening.

"What's happening?!" I yelled.

"You are thinking about betraying the garden, Nicolette! It can sense it!"

My grandmother rose to her feet and quickly made her way over to the tree, caressing it and whispering. The buzzing subsided and the glowing returned to the soft pulse that had been prevalent only moments earlier. My grandmother turned to me. She was incredibly angry. I could see it written across her wrinkles and frown, with an intensity in her eyes like a fire ready to consume the world.

"Nicolette! When I die, I will be leaving all of this to you. You will be responsible for maintaining this secret! It is all about balance and sacrifice! If we betray the garden's secret and the outside tears down these walls, then there is nothing that can stop this world from completely taking over ours! I may be a selfish old woman who does not want her property taken away! But I am also not a fool! I know that keeping this sister rift a secret is what is keeping it from spilling out of here!"

Whispers took to the air. I could not make out what they were saying. But my grandmother somehow understood this language that now surrounded us.

"They are displeased that you have snuck in here, child! We must go at once!"

My grandmother quickly grabbed my hand and started to pull me behind her. She moved as fast as her feeble steps would allow her to, trying to get back to the garden's entrance as quickly as she could. But it was far, and the garden was now terribly angry. The skies began to dim, and then from the shadows, draped in darkness, the sound of gigantic wings started to echo through the air.

"Oh no," my grandmother whispered. "He knows."

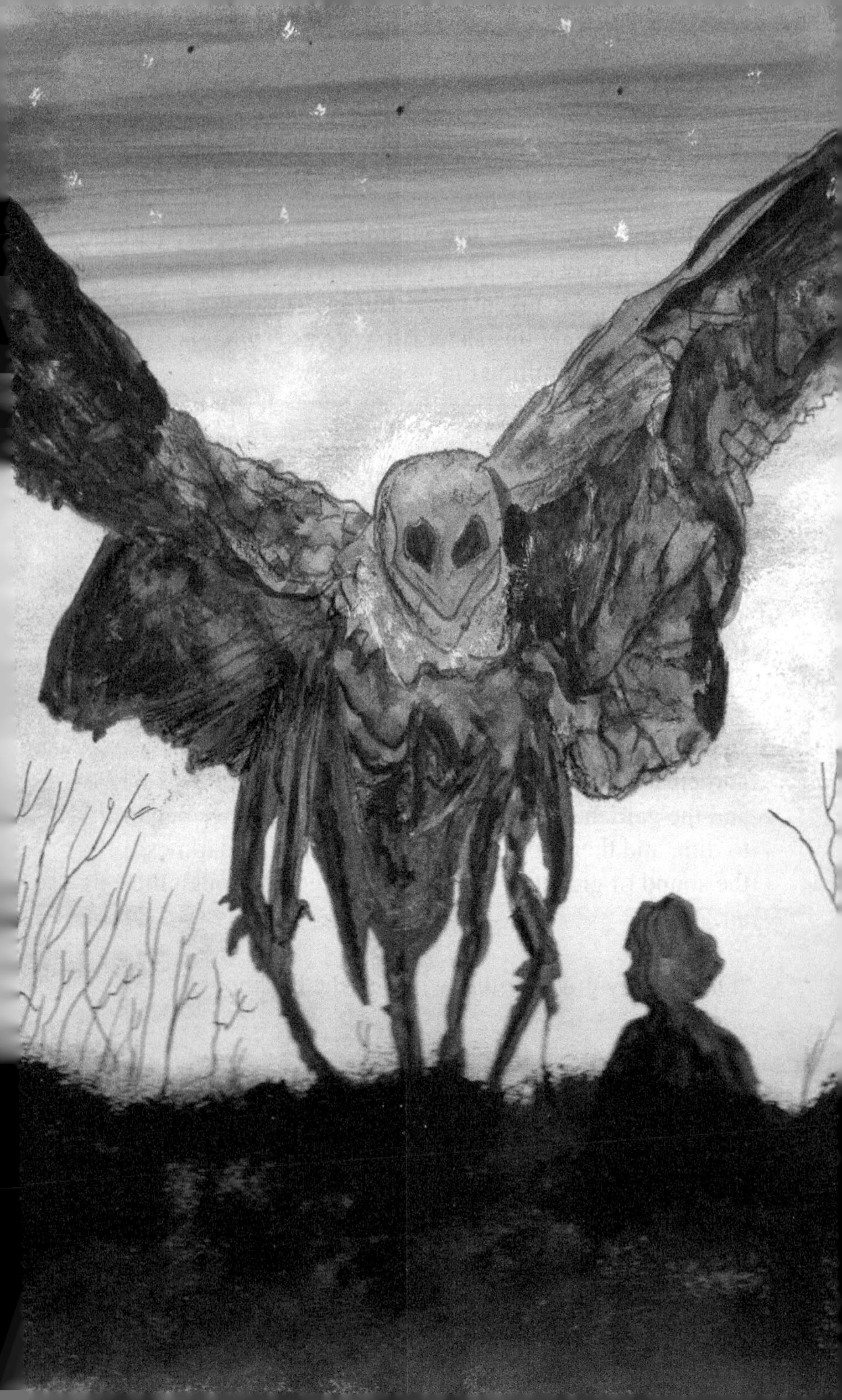

~ Chapter Five: The Sacrifice ~

The horrifying creature before us was nothing like I had ever seen. A giant moth with the face of a ghost, hazy and glowing with a purple tint. It slowly set down in front of us, perching itself upon the dense soil. Its wings stirred the air and created a stale breeze and a foul stench. Its head cocked back and forth, urgently perceiving our presence, and moving towards us. My grandmother quickly stood in front of me like a shield, trying to hide me. She then raised her voice and yelled at the creature.

"Leave us alone! We have an agreement!"

The creature started to violently hiss and shake at us. But soon the hisses that erupted from its voice turned to haunting words. I had never heard of a creature from the rift that could speak like us. It was as if its voice surrounded us and planted each word deep into our minds. As if something about being here within these garden walls had merged our two languages into one. Perhaps all the creatures here shared the same tongue. For all I knew, we were the ones speaking *their* language.

"You have brought a stranger into our sacred realm. The garden has told me that they intend to reveal us! Furthermore, the agreement of which you speak only extends to one soul! You!" hissed the creature.

"She is here by mistake! Only curiosity has led her steps to this place! Please leave her be! I will take her to the other side of this garden wall immediately!" screamed my grandmother.

"So that she may betray the agreement and bring forth an army to crumble these walls and attack us?" the creature asked.

"I promise that she will not! She is only but a child! I will explain our agreement to her!" my grandmother argued.

I feared for my life at that moment. I could feel the winds shift and turn away from the beauty that I had just witnessed. The stained-glass sky now went black with only the soft glimmer of once-bright stars. A fog gradually rolled in and began to choke the air. Then the creature grew silent as it looked deep into my grandmother's eyes. It then looked to me. Its purple hue shifted to that of a soft mossy green, and the air became less stale.

"I am only a soldier for him. I am sorry, but you have broken my master's agreement, so I must collect a soul on this night. And I must not fail. However, you may plead your case to the one known as Erra if you so desire."

"But Erra is a heartless monster. If he knows the child is here, he will surely consume her," said my grandmother.

"This is true. Nevertheless… *if* you plead your case to him, it may allow time for the child to escape. For I will make sure that the garden does not spread the word of her presence, so long as I leave here with a soul."

"I understand," my grandmother replied.

Her voice sounded strained like she was choking on her own reply to this terrifying creature. She then looked at me, tears in her eyes. A subtle smile crept across her clearly distraught face, pushing her ever-present wrinkles up towards her grieving eyes.

"Nicolette. I must leave you now," she said softly.

"No! Grandmother! I am sorry I followed you here! I am sorry I had thoughts of revealing this secret! But I swear that I will not! I swear that I will never enter these walls again!" I pleaded.

The creature gradually lifted off the ground, hovering in place as its massive wings swooped through the air. It started to approach my grandmother and me. Its daunting presence blocked out what light was left by the fading stars.

"You were just being a child," my grandmother explained.

The creature's wings flapped slowly, beating like a drum. Like a war drum being struck across a battlefield.

Woosh, woosh, woosh.

"And I will not hold ill will for a child simply being what they are," my grandmother continued as the winged creature grew closer and closer.

Woosh, woosh, woosh.

"Now, I need you to listen to me very carefully, Nicolette. I want you to leave this garden. I want you to find the gate, lock it behind you, and never let another soul beyond these walls!"

Woosh, woosh, woosh.

"You cannot allow these two worlds to merge!"

She pulled the key from around her neck and handed it to me. Tears streamed down my face. What had I done?

"Promise me!" she yelled as the winged shadow hovered just above her.

I did not know how to respond. In fear, I shook in silent tongues and pale skin.

"Promise me!" she screamed again as the creature's talons slowly wrapped around her arms.

"I…" I softly started.

But before any more words could escape my trembling lips, the creature clenched hold of my grandmother with its talons and instantly whisked her away, far off into the sky, disappearing into the night. She did not scream or cry. The air just fell silent. The only sound remaining was the soft whimper of my sadness as I fell to the ground and sobbed. I had now lost everything. I had no home. I had no family. It was my fault that the winged soldier of the realm had taken her. I clung to my breath as it moved erratically and sharply, causing me to tire and fall victim to my own panic and fear. The garden went dark as I crumbled to my side. And exhausted, there I slept.

My dreams were an oddity on that cursed night. As I slept upon the garden's dense floor, I was visited not by nightmares or visions of loss, but by a journey laced with memories from a world that I had never imagined.

In this dream, my name was Laura, like the girl from that book that my mother had read to me many times. And just like that book, I found myself in a strange new world. I was on a journey with my sister, Mary, as we searched for our dog, Jack. This journey was held by nervous steps. The days and nights seemed to blend together, creating a constant stream of moments that were impossible to count. Along the way, we were met with curious creatures and moments of great challenge. Some of these creatures were kind, others mysterious, and one, whose face we could not see, was terrifying. But they all led us to Jack. To us saving him. It was like we were destined to be there. But at the end of our journey, we found a rift. There was no rift in that book though. And as often happens within dreams, the real world began to collide with the stories of comfort that my mother had once read to me. I was scared. But then a voice that spoke in riddles comforted me and begged me to move forward. I let go of Jack and Mary, and I stepped inside the rift.

Beyond my steps, I found a world that words could never describe. A world of colors and creatures too breathtaking to comprehend. The creatures were consumed by a mighty war. A faceless enemy, and a rift that was trying to deplete their world of all life. Sadness hovered over this place. A chaotic existence that had been misunderstood. Then something happened. Something terrifying. Something that required great bravery. Something important. Although, I could not remember what this something was. But within a dream, nothing is as simple as linear movement.

The next thing I knew, I was greeted with open arms by my parents. I called them Ma and Pa, just like Laura did. They were alive and well. They held me closely. We were back in our house, but the walls were no longer rubble, and the windows were no longer cracked. The city was no longer on fire. The streets were no longer covered in the bodies of those who had been lost. It was as if nothing had occurred, and the world was as it was before. I was trapped in a fool's dream.

We played games together, and ate meals, and read books. We laughed, living within the small moments of peace and silence that were now prevalent. And all the horrors that had erupted from The Viridian Rift were simply a forgotten memory. A nightmare from a distant past that only existed in a fictional future. This was a beautiful dream. So vivid and so kind.

I awoke, still on the garden floor. I was cold and shivering. Gone was the touch of a fool's dream. I was that fool. I slowly sat up, looking around at the garden. How would I ever get out of here? I clutched the key that rested around my neck. I felt its warmth. I could almost hear my grandmother's voice telling me to leave.

Instructing me to lock away this world and never return. The garden gates called to me with their song.

   I stood tall, still clutching the key. But then I stopped before stepping. Something wasn't right. Nothing was waiting for me back there. Why would anyone return? Why would anyone want to return to a land with no one to love? My dream whispered. It was starting to fade, but I could not shake the feeling that leaving this place was not my true path. My grandmother could still be alive. I would travel across this garden, and just like Laura, I would explore this strange world. I would save my grandmother. I would fulfill my dream's destiny. I knew where I had to go.

   I heard my father's voice. A distant memory from brighter days. A summer morning, and a trip to the park, when I had begged him not to remove the training wheels from my bicycle, for I was scared of falling.

"If it's too easy, Nicolette, you'll never accomplish anything," he said with a little wink.

   I had trusted him, and the next thing I knew I was sent flying down the path, laughing all the while, freer than I had ever felt. I had to remove the training wheels.

   Without hesitation, I ripped the key from my neck and threw it away, into the shadows. I could not give myself an easy path. So, I took a deep breath and turned away from the gate's direction. Why was I so anxious to follow a fool's dream over reality? A hunger, a feeling, an aching. A hope that could be felt throughout my bones.

So, with a vision coursing through my veins, and my father's voice cheering me on, I set off in an unknown direction. My heart led my step. And even though I did not know what was before my path, I knew that it was my destiny to seek out this other rift and hopefully find my grandmother along the way.

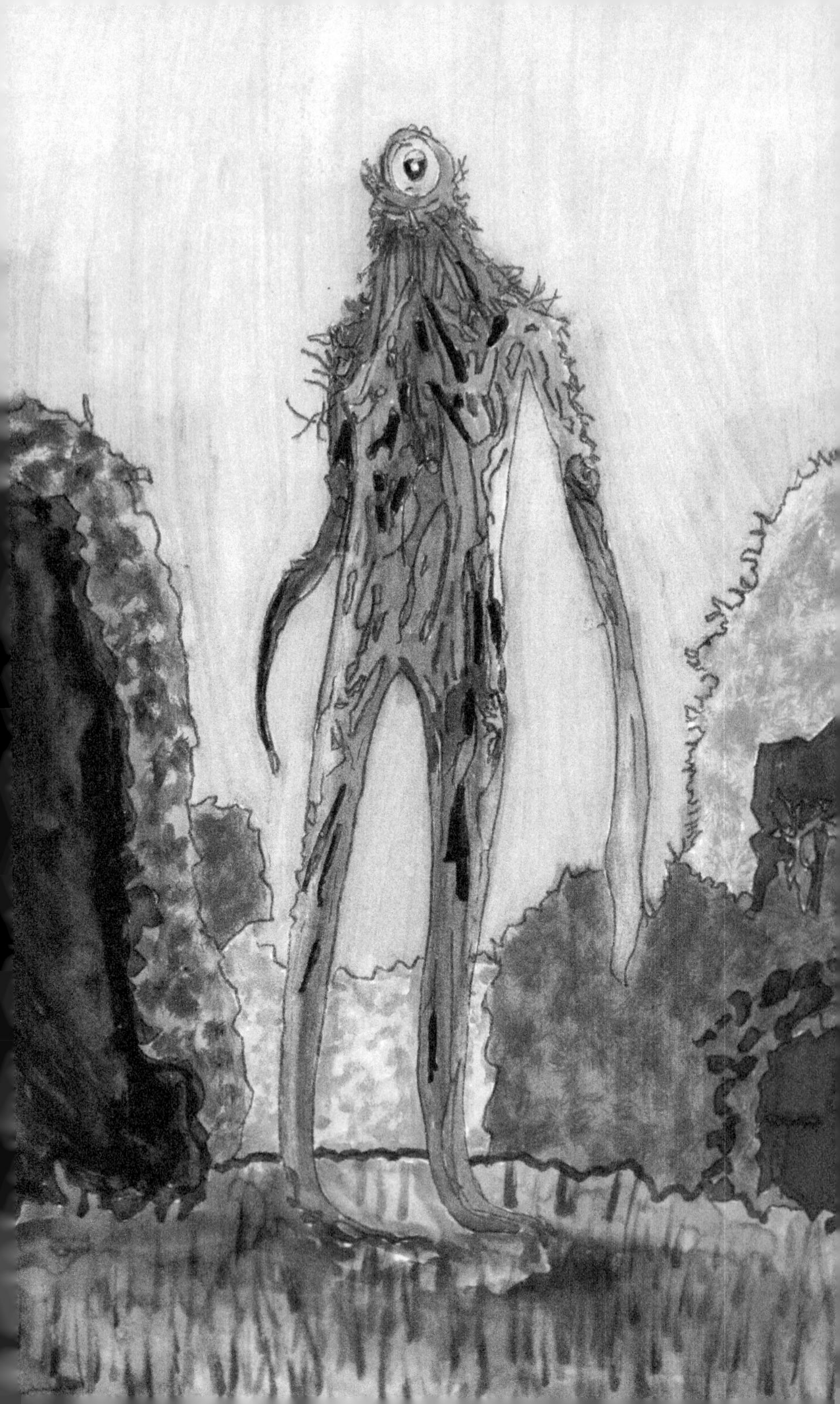

~ Chapter Six: An Unpronounceable Name ~

The sun started to make its way high above the garden walls, shining down upon this strange place. In the daytime the light shone through the sky like a prism, casting various shadows, colors, and reflections everywhere that could be seen. The plants were something to behold. Each shimmering and vibrating with the echo of an unseen reality, as if the rift had not only crept inside our world but also manipulated and changed it. The flowers looked familiar, but their shapes and colors were all vaguely different. Something that reminded me of how things ought to be, but were not.

As I made my way towards the unknown, I began to feel hungry. My stomach rumbled and reminded me that I was still in need of nourishment. A long journey begs for sustenance. I couldn't help but think about the biscuits that Elisa had made for me. Their golden crust and buttery flavor wrapped up in every bite. Even the subpar meals that Mr. Oswald had prepared for me sounded amazing at the moment. But everywhere I looked, I could not tell what was edible or alive. Plants seemed to move with no breeze, and I could not bring myself to try and eat anything that might be alive or have the same intelligence as I.

Suddenly, I heard a rustle of movement from a nearby bush, as if a mighty carnivore were hiding just behind it. I swore I could hear heavy breathing and growling from just beyond my sight. It was hard to tell if I was just imagining things though. When trapped in an alternate and eternal world beyond the walls of what you've always known as reality, it is easy to get swept up by random creaks and whispers.

Then, from out of nowhere, the bush that I had thought was hiding a mighty carnivore, stood up. It towered above me, stoic and silent. No longer just a random piece of shrubbery, but a creature the likes of which I had never seen. Their one giant eye, looking down at me curiously. I felt the urge to run away, but I stood as tall as I could, even with such a tiny stature. I had to be brave, for this was only the first step of many, and I would surely meet many more creatures as I traveled this path.

"Hello," I said while trying to perform my most proper curtsy.

The creature bent down towards me. Was it about to devour me? Should I have run away at its first appearance?

"You… are a strange little thing," the creature said in a soft voice.

I was no longer shocked to hear a creature from the rift speak in my world's tongue. Something that was apparently quite common here. Their voice almost sounded like it was trying to make itself heard from deep beneath an ocean's waves. Muffled and soft, yet still clear enough to understand. I was frozen by the moment, unsure of how to reply.

"Are you filled with mush?" the creature asked as they took their branch-like arm and gently poked at my belly, making me giggle.

"My name is, Nicolette," I replied softly, trying to hide my nervousness. "And I guess you could say that, yes, I *am* filled with mush. All of my kind are."

The creature looked me up and down, taking note of my size and appearance. I was not sure of their intentions as of yet, so I continued to stand tall, ready to run away at a moment's notice.

"My name is EEEEHAGSHDSGDYSGYUCDAIDYYYY!"

The creature's reply was almost deafening. Their name had been announced by way of a screeching, screaming, howling sound. The kind of sound that made my heart leap from my chest and my palms cover my ears. It was so loud and sudden that it sent me to my knees. I slowly stood back up, trying to compose myself.

"Well, I don't think I can pronounce that. Is there something… shorter? Like a nickname or something?" I asked.

"The old woman called me Bonbon," the creature replied.

I couldn't help but chuckle at such a silly name.

"I believe the old woman, of which you speak, is my grandmother," I explained.

Bonbon looked around for a moment as if expecting my grandmother to pop out from behind a bush and try to scare us.

"Where is she now?" asked Bonbon. "I would quite like to say hello."

My smile disappeared. I did not enjoy sharing bad news, so the words juggled around recklessly within my thoughts before cascading out of my mouth.

"She was stolen away in the middle of the night by a giant moth-like creature, and taken to something named, Erra," I finally replied.

"Oh, my!" Bonbon yelled. "This is not good, Nicolas!"

"My name is, Nicolette."

"That's what I said."

"No! You said Nicolas!" I argued.

"Yes, exactly what I said. The same thing."

"It is *clearly* not the same thing! Only the beginning is the same! Everything after was different!"

"But the beginning is the most important part," argued Bonbon.

Exacerbated, I gave up on trying to have the creature with an unpronounceable name try and pronounce mine.

After all, they must have butchered my grandmother's name if she had chosen the silly nickname of *Bonbon* for this truly irritating, yet somehow endearing, creature.

"Fine. It's fine," I said calmly. "Call me whatever you want. It's really not important. Do you know where my grandmother was taken?"

"If I were to guess… my guess would be… no more than a guess… and no more than a guess… is less than a truth…"

"What?!" I replied.

"Exactly," whispered Bonbon.

I was speechless. I was most likely not going to get anywhere in my conversation with Bonbon. They clearly knew nothing and were not going to be of any help.

"I must be going," I said curtly, before marching away, deeper into the unknown.

My belly was still rumbling, and my strength and hope were starting to wane. Perhaps I shouldn't have thrown the key away. What a foolish thing to do. But I had no choice now, I had to keep moving, and staying around here, in the company of Bonbon, was obviously not going to help me whatsoever.

"Wait!" yelled Bonbon. "Little Nicolas! I do not know where your grandmother is. But the Elders might!"

I abruptly stopped, turned around, and made my way back over to the giant.

"The Elders?" I asked.

"Yes. Yes. They were the first ones through the rift to make a home in this strange garden. They know this bizarre world better than any of us! So, they may be able to help…"

My stomach growled loudly.

"… and even perhaps get you something to eat."

"Well, why didn't you start with that?!" I asked. "I'm starving!"

"Very well. Then you must follow me, little one. But stay close! It is a treacherous journey! With plenty of places to trip and fall!"

"How far away is it?" I nervously asked.

Bonbon slowly turned and pointed to a tree no more than fifteen yards away.

"Right behind that tree," Bonbon said.

I rolled my eyes.

"That is not very far at all."

"It is when your roots are sewn to the ground."

Bonbon gently pulled up their legs from the ground. Roots snapped like twigs, sending dirt flying in all directions. With each step they took, their hanging roots would fuse to the soil and then have to be broken again. Repeatedly, the slowest steps I had ever seen. And those fifteen yards seemed to take an eternity to travel. But after what felt like hours, we finally turned the corner around the tree and were greeted by the sight of a massive church-like structure. One that resembled a cathedral but appeared to be made out of morphed and disfigured trees. The walls were covered in moss and leaves, and the whole thing shimmered in the sun with a hazy glow.

"Is this the rift?" I asked.

Bonbon laughed loudly.

"No. No. Silly, little, Nicolas. This is just the structure where the Elders reside. Believe me. When you see the rift, you will know. Your words will be reduced to a whisper by its beauty."

We approached a pair of mighty doors. They looked as if they had not been touched in a lifetime. Grown over with plants and covered in soil.

"You must be the one who knocks," instructed Bonbon. "For this is where I leave you, little one."

"But..." I started.

"I will only slow your pace, and I am much too scared to help you face the evils that lie ahead."

I realized that the tone that I had taken with Bonbon was just due to my hunger. I felt bad for how I had talked to them, considering all they were trying to do was help me.

"I am also scared, Bonbon. But if you were by my side, I would be far less scared."

I had pleaded my case to the gentle giant. But I knew in my heart that I was not going to change their fear with my child's words.

"Too scared," Bonbon whispered.

Then before I could plead my case further, Bonbon slowly began to make their way back to where we had been. I appreciated the company on that fifteen-yard journey. But I had hoped that Bonbon would have remained in my company for longer than a stroll.

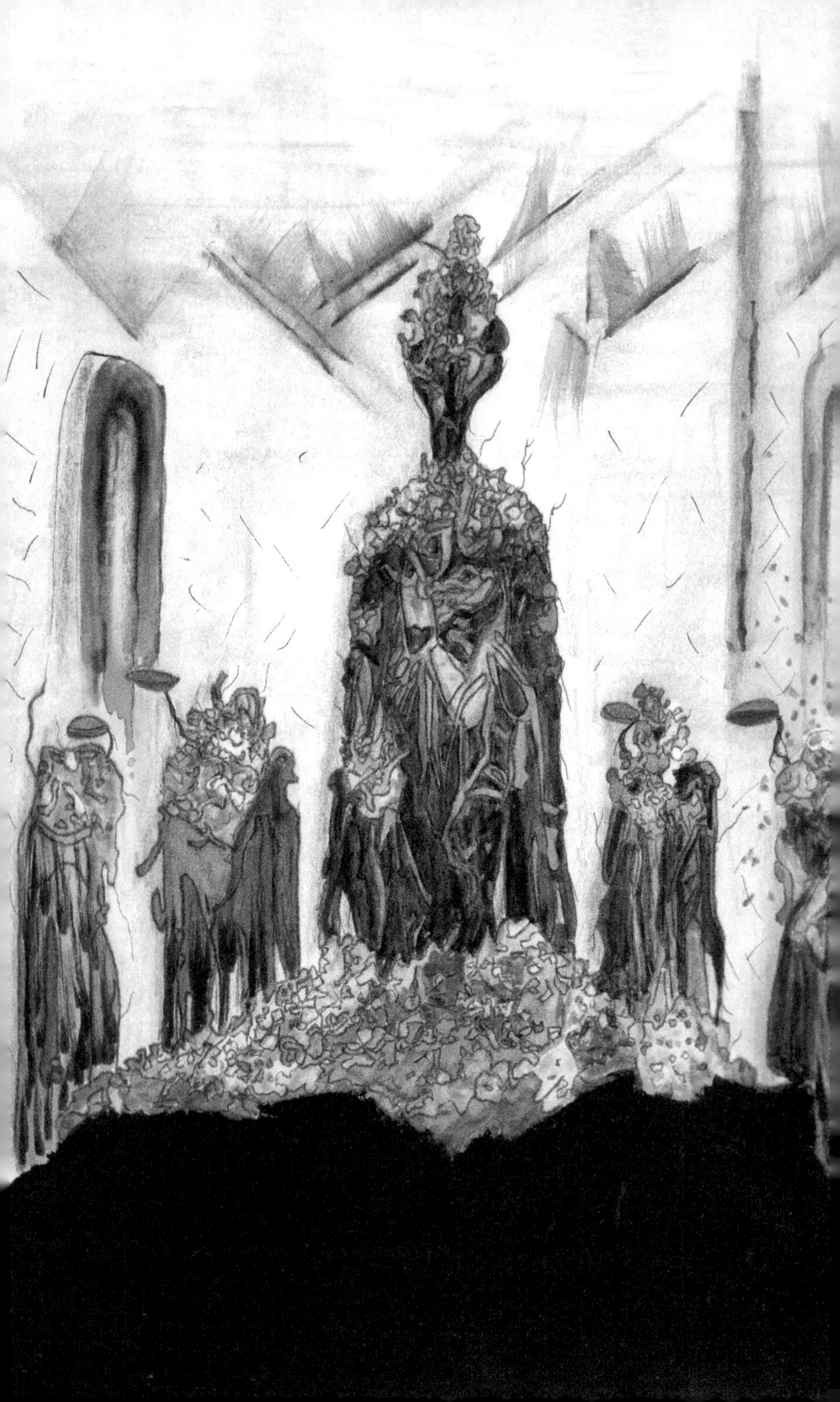

~ Chapter Seven: The Elders ~

I pounded against the massive doors that stood much taller than any entrance I had ever seen. The sound made by my fists reverberated against the day's silent backdrop as if it were the only sound in the world. I waited for the echoes to fade away, being once again left in the company of silence, and then went to knock once more. But just as I was about to do so, the doors slowly started to open. A hiss of fog and light erupted from behind them, and I was forced to step backward out of fear and instinct.

"You may enter!" a voice yelled from within the mysterious chamber.

Deep breath. I had to be brave. One foot in front of the other, I walked into the unknown. The darkness reminded me of a canvas from an unfinished painting. Only fog and color, with no real definition. I pushed through, finding myself in a grand hall. Its walls were filled with what looked to be shards of glass, like a million mirrors that had been broken and then hung up like works of art. The shards reflected various hues of purples and whites all around the room, creating an aura that was incredibly disorienting.

This hall was *far* bigger than what I had imagined when looking at it from the outside. Suddenly, the shapes of several strange creatures began to appear from behind the lights and fog. They surrounded a large bushel of colorful flowers in the middle of the floor, attached to its base with their roots intertwined. Creatures that, just like Bonbon, seemed to be made of plants. Four of them were gathered behind what appeared to be their great leader. Those four all wore strange glowing objects from their heads, like white jellyfish that floated in the air just above them. One single tentacle was all that connected these jellyfish-like halos to them, pulsating, and humming with a soft melody, harmonizing with one another. Their leader stood taller than the rest, twice their size, adorned with purple flowers across their brow. Like a crown that might be worn by royalty.

"Come closer, child," the leader instructed with a voice that sounded almost identical to that of Bonbon's.

I cautiously approached the Elders, trying not to be afraid. Had I not just met Bonbon, I would surely be shivering with fright and fret, and running for the still-open doors. But the warm glow from their existence challenged my perception of what I had thought possible, lulling me in, and making me feel at peace to be near them. Like a gentle song or a summer night, I felt safe.

"What is your name?" the leader asked.

"My name is Nicolette."

"It is good to meet you, Natasha. I am known as Fonfroo," they replied.

"I..." I started.

"What is it?" Fonfroo asked as I debated correcting them on my name.

"Nothing. It is nothing," I said with a slight giggle.

Surely something about my name confused this realm's creatures. Perplexing as it was, I chose to simply ignore their grammatical shortcomings and get to the whole reason why I had walked those arduous fifteen yards.

"Bonbon suggested that I meet with you," I said.

"Ah. And for what reason did Bonbon feel that us meeting you would be beneficial?"

"For one, I need something to eat. I am *very* hungry, and he told me that you might be able to feed me?"

Without hesitation, Fonfroo pulled a glowing purple fruit from the top of their head and handed it to me.

"Are you sure I can eat this?" I asked suspiciously.

"Most certainly. The fruit grown by our kind is known to be some of the most delicious in all of existence."

My stomach growled at me once more, practically begging me to try this strange fruit. What did I have to lose? I was already lost beyond the walls of the world to which I belonged, my grandmother had been taken captive, and I had been stumbling around with no real direction for what felt like ages but was only hours. I shrugged my shoulders and then bit into the fruit. It was soft and juicy like a giant cherry. Sweet like honey, with a slightly sour taste to it. I couldn't help but devour it in a matter of a few seconds. It was delicious and I was starving.

"Thank you very much!" I said while wiping my face with my sleeve.

The Elders all proceeded to laugh in unison.

"What? What is it?" I asked.

"Your face is now the same color as the fruit," Fonfroo laughed. "You are not very careful with your hungry bites, are you?"

I caught a glimpse of myself in one of the wall's many reflections. The Elders had been true to their word: my face was now bright purple. The juice from that delicious fruit had stained me, making me look like a giant grape. I was reminded of when I would eat too many blueberries and my mother would tease me by calling me her little *kingfisher*. A peculiar-looking bird that was often bright blue. I couldn't help but smile. I wondered what she would call me if she could see me now. I wiped my face off again until much of the purple had vanished, and then I turned my attention back to the Elders.

"Is my face cleaner now, Mr. Fonfroo?" I asked.

"Yes, yes. Much better," they replied. "What else might we be able to do for you, Natasha?"

"Well... I need to find my grandmother. Her name is Madam Duplantier. I am sure you know of her."

"Oh yes. She has spent much of her time visiting with us and enjoying our fruit. Where is she?" Fonfroo asked.

"She was stolen away last night, by a giant winged creature and taken to the one known as Erra."

The Elders all gasped, and a coldness crept over the hall, dulling the bright purple lights, and immediately making my breath visible. Something about that name had brought forth a winter's touch and exposed the elder's greatest fears.

"Erra is truly a monster," revealed Fonfroo. "If he has taken your grandmother… then I am afraid that we must fear the worst."

Surely there had to be a way to rescue her. I would not give up on her just because the name of this monster frightened the Elders.

"No. That is not good enough," I said. "Tell me about this monster so I can face him."

"Are you sure you want to face Erra?" asked a clearly hesitant Fonfroo.

"To save my grandmother? Yes, I am positive!"

"Very well. Erra is a criminal from our realm that escaped to this one through the rift. He has been trying to take control of everything within these walls since arriving. But recently, your grandmother had convinced him to leave us all alone, so long as any agreements made, remained unbroken."

"So, me being here must have broken the agreement he had with my grandmother."

"He takes all agreements *very* seriously," replied Fonfroo.

I still had to try and save her. I'd not thrown the key into the shadows and embarked upon this journey with no purpose. No, I had to try and free my grandmother since I was the reason why she had been stolen away in the first place.

"I have no choice but to face Erra. I must know where I can find him," I said.

"Erra is out beyond the shimmering forest, at the edge of the great dunes. Halfway between this place and the great rift."

"I do not want to get lost, and I may also need help to defeat him and free my grandmother. Will any of you accompany me?"

The Elders all grew quiet, and the air once again went cold. Just like Bonbon, they wore fear across their brows.

"We cannot go with you, for we are far too slow. By the time we arrived, it would be much too late, and I fear that your grandmother would be no more," Fonfroo explained.

"Lies! You are all just scared of him!" I yelled.

"If fear is our choice, then you must respect that," Fonfroo replied.

"But how am I supposed to defeat this monster?! How am I supposed to find him, let alone fight him?!"

"I know not how you are supposed to defeat him. But we will send out a call to all those that wish to help. The creatures of the forest. They will not help you fight him, but they will gladly guide your way."

"But how?" I asked.

"With a path made of colors."

Then the Elders all looked towards the heavens and exhaled a song that rattled the walls and shook the ground. Like a choir singing a hymnal, their joyous notes filled the air with music. Then from the ground sprouted a single yellow flower planted directly at my feet. Then another... and another. They created a glowing path that moved away from them, out of the grand hall, and towards Erra. The flowers bounced and shone with a kaleidoscope of colors that lit up every step I took with a different hue. After starting to follow this path of flowers, I took two steps and then stopped, turning back to the Elders.

"I do not know how I will defeat this monster alone. I am scared," I confessed.

I could see that had the Elders not also been paralyzed by their own fears, they would help me defeat this monster and free this place of his tyranny.

"Try and not be frightened, little one. Perhaps the love you carry for your grandmother will be enough to defeat Erra."

"Thank you for feeding me and guiding my path," I said with a nervous smile. "I am sorry that I got angry with you all."

Fonfroo snatched another fruit from their head, then slowly extended their arm like a root across the grand hall, handing it to me.

"One for the road, my new friend."

"Thank you, Fonfroo."

I took the fruit and began my journey across this path of colors. Not knowing how I would defeat the monster that held my grandmother captive but being aware that I was her only hope.

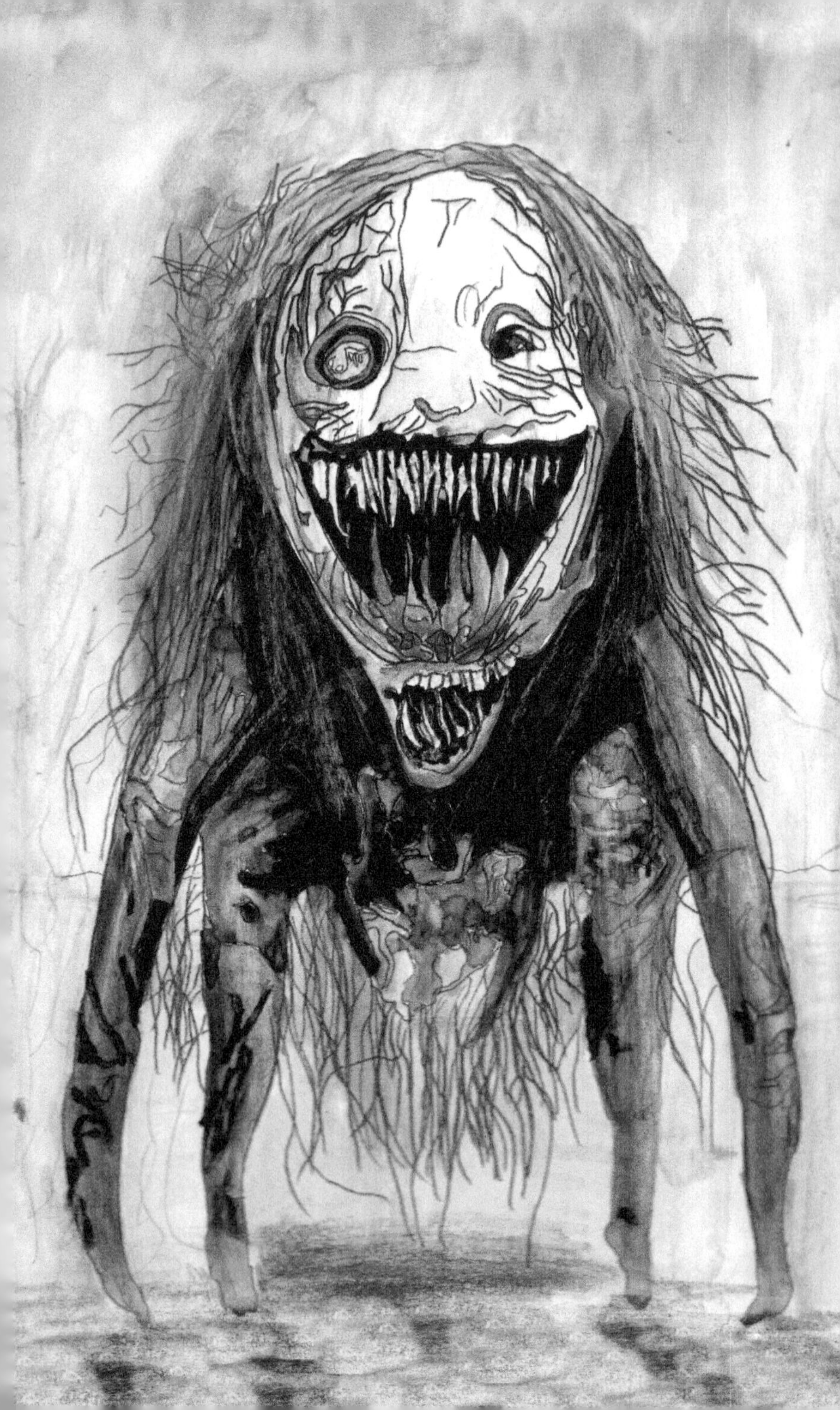

~ Chapter Eight: Erra ~

I traveled that glowing path, laid before me by the Elders. With every step I took, more flowers erupted from the soil, directly in front of me, guiding my steady step and decided direction. I could still hear the Elders' song echoing through the air, bouncing off the prisms of color that filled the sky. It was now midday, and as I traveled across this strange place, I found myself basking in its beauty. The realm within these walls was both magnificent and seemingly endless. I could not believe that all of this was just within the garden. The world from the other side of the rift bleeding through and stretching space and time into this magical place.

Along this journey, I bore witness to many villages filled with creatures just like Fonfroo and Bonbon. Tiny little towns with small huts and gardens of purple fruits. They all waved at me as I passed them by. As if they knew the purpose I carried within my steps. Then they too sang to the heavens with the same song that I had heard from the Elders. They carried that song with every step of this path, cheering me on with their melodic breath.

As the day began to fade, I found myself once again hungry. So, I found a spot of soft grasses to rest for a moment and indulge in the fruit that Fonfroo had given to me. Delicious. As I finished eating it, I could hear the flowers that covered this path all come to life and start to giggle at me and my purple face. I chuckled along with them. I couldn't help it. A moment of joy within an anxious quest. If my grandmother's life was not in my hands, I could just rest here forever under these stained-glass skies. But enough rest. I had to press on. I had to save her. So, I rose to my feet and wiped the purple from my face before continuing with my journey.

Eventually, just before nightfall, I emerged from the edge of the forest and found myself somewhere new. It was unlike anywhere I had been before. A small patch of land that was surrounded by dead trees, harsh soil, and broken limbs, at the mouth of a desert. Knowing that the trees could walk and talk here, it was as if I was being asked to journey through a field of corpses and stale death. There was no denying, this was a graveyard. A desperate breath, where the air grew tired and sad. So thick that I could barely breathe. And then, the path stopped and the yellow flowers beneath me all whimpered and died before my eyes. I had arrived. I was where I was meant to be. The sun was almost gone now, leaving me surrounded by shadows and fear. Then I heard a raspy and labored breath from just beyond where I could see.

"Hello?!" I yelled.

I looked around. I could not see any monsters here. I did not see my grandmother. I just heard the tortured breath of something unknown, gasping from just beyond my sight like it was about to take its last breath at any moment.

"Grandmother?! Are you here?!" I asked.

Then, from the shadows, a monster appeared, grotesque and polluted by everything evil. Like some type of insect towering over me, covered with long tangled hair, black eyes, and two mouths stacked atop one another. The words did not exist to properly capture this horror before my shivered gaze. I froze in silence as the beast then began to speak. Not just from one of its mouths, but from both. One that was so incredibly low, that it immediately took my breath away, practically bringing me to tears with only a few words. The second voice was much higher and had a bitter bite to it, like the taste of vinegar put into a vomited chorus of sounds. It just seemed to echo the first voice, reinforcing whatever had just been said. But they were of one mind. A sick and deranged mind that was the portrait of fear. Like every unkind word and pointless death that had ever been, were all at once pushed through the words of these whispers.

"We… had an agreement. *(An agreement, yes,)*" said the beast.

I tried to speak, but every bit of bravery that I'd carried thus far had been swallowed up by the sight of this monster, whom I could only assume held the name of Erra.

"Your presence here violated that agreement, filthy child! (*Filthy little child!)*" the monster roared.

I could not face this monster. I jumped away and immediately turned, running back towards the forest's embrace. I had no weapons. I had no bravery. What could a child, such as I, ever hope to do that would vanquish something this frightening? I started to run towards the tree line, as Erra laughed loudly. Almost in my grasp. Almost to safety. My grandmother was probably dead, and I did not want to also die under these stained-glass skies.

Then I heard it. A sound that stopped my hurried feet and made me turn back around towards the monster. The sound I heard was of my grandmother crying. But her voice was muffled as if hidden somewhere. Then I realized where she was. She was in Erra's belly. And as he laughed at me and my cowardice, my grandmother wept from behind his rows and rows of sharpened teeth. Her voice gave way to my bravery.

"Let her go!" I screamed.

"No! I will not! *(Never!)*" shrieked Erra. "And if you do not run away, and insist on seeing her, then you can join her! *(Join! Join! Join!)*"

Then a long tongue erupted from Erra's larger mouth. It was black and forked at the end like a serpent. It even moved like a snake as it charged towards me, across the graves of trees, finding my weathered step, and wrapping itself around my legs. It pulled me from my feet and forced me to the ground, knocking the wind from my lungs and scraping my knees. Then it started to pull me towards Erra. Closer and closer. What was I to do? As soon as I got close enough to stare this monster in the eyes, it came to me. Without hesitation, I pulled the aigrette, which my grandmother had given to me, from my hair. Those three feathers and a blue jewel, attached to sharp pins. Then just before he could consume me, I jabbed Erra in the chest with the aigrette. He immediately dropped me and screamed in pain. Then I pulled myself to my feet, grabbed the aigrette, and yanked down on it, ripping the monster open and spilling a cloud of black smoke and silver blood across the ground. My grandmother fell out of the monster and gasped for air.

"Grandmother!"

"What are you doing here?! I told you to leave!" she yelled as fear filled her eyes.

"It's okay, grandmother. I've defeated Erra. We're safe now."

But then Erra started to laugh and stitch himself back together. Tiny black threads that moved like thousands of snakes, coiling around each other, and pulling this monster's slain pieces back to whole. My attack had not killed the monster, just made him angrier. My grandmother got to her feet as quickly as she could.

"We must run!" she screamed.

We tried to get away from Erra, back to the forest and its safety. But as we quickened our steps, it became obvious that the monster was just toying with us. It scaled the dead trees and lunged from branch to branch, always ahead of us and blocking our path, laughing all the while. But just as all hope had faded, and Erra had us both cornered, a deafening song filled the air, and the ground began to sprout grass and flowers of every color.

"What is happening?! *(What is happening?!)*" screamed Erra.

Then, from out of the forest, appeared Bonbon, Fonfroo, the Elders, and a small army of creatures just like them.

"Leave Nancy and her grandmother alone!" yelled Fonfroo.

Then the army of creatures charged at Erra. He tried to get away from them, but their vines whipped at him and wrapped around his legs, pulling him to the ground. Erra screamed while trying to bite at the vines with both of his mouths, whipping his forked tongue back and forth. But he was no match for the strength brought forth by these numbers. They pulled the monster down, deep into the ground, burying him below the surface, and locking him away forever. So deep, that even if he could manage to find his breath, he would never be able to find his way back up to the surface.

The creatures all pulled their vines back to their sides and then turned to myself and my grandmother.

"You're all here!" I exclaimed.

"Yes, we are, child," said Fonfroo.

"But... I thought it was *too* far and you were *too* scared to ever help me face Erra?"

"If a child filled with mush can be brave enough to face a monster like that all on her own, then we should not have any excuses," replied Bonbon.

"But then how did you get here so quickly? How did you untether your roots from the soil as you took each step?" I asked.

"While fear may slow one's step, bravery will hasten it like a strong wind," replied Fonfroo.

"Plus, we took a shortcut," added Bonbon.

I laughed at Bonbon before turning my attention back towards my grandmother. She was alive. I had helped to save her. My happiness at seeing her unharmed was more joy than I had felt in an exceedingly long time. With tears in my eyes, I hugged her tightly, never wanting to let go.

"You saved me, Nicolette," she said.

"It wasn't just me. All your friends helped," I said.

My grandmother looked at the creatures of the forest.

"Thank you all for helping to save me! For helping my granddaughter find her way! I had feared that I would be forced to live out the rest of my days in Erra's smoked-filled belly! But you were all so brave!"

"It was your granddaughter that inspired our bravery, ma'am," said Fonfroo.

"Well, nevertheless, I must still thank you. After all, we would have both been gobbled up by that monster had you not come to our rescue."

"Our pleasure, my friend," started Fonfroo. "Plus, now we are all free of Erra and his tyrannical terror!"

The creatures all cheered loudly. Then Fonfroo plucked a couple of pieces of fruit from his brow to give to us and thanked us both before journeying back towards the forest. The small army followed behind, leaving only me, my grandmother, and Bonbon.

"Well, we should make our way back to the gate. Hopefully, Mr. Oswald is not too worried about us," said my grandmother.

I had almost forgotten.

"We can't," I said softly.

"Why not?" she asked.

"Because… I threw the key away," I sobbingly confessed.

"Why would you do such a thing?!" my grandmother yelled.

She sounded angry. And why shouldn't she be? Our only way out of this place was tossed aside like it was worthless.

"I wanted to give myself no other choice but to save you," I blurted out.

My grandmother's anger seemed to vanish in a flash, and she smiled at me. Even though she was clearly irritated at now being trapped inside these walls, she could see that I had chosen against the sting of failure. A foolish choice that begged to be admired.

"Very well," my grandmother said.

She then took a seat next to an old tree. She sat silently for a few moments, deep in thought, juggling our options.

"No time for tears," I whispered to myself.

I wiped the tears from my eyes and went to sit beside her, silent, mirroring her focused demeanor.

"Without the key, I am afraid we are trapped here," she said.

"Is there nothing we can do?" I asked.

"Our future is now in the hands of fate," she replied.

Then, as if summoned by our predicament, a shadow arose from the ground and presented itself to us as a cloaked figure, tall and thin, with one arm that elongated all the way to the ground like a walking stick. We all jumped back, ready to fight if needed. But this stranger did not appear to be dangerous. After we had stood our ground for a moment or two, the stranger spoke, like a soft wind trapped in a mighty storm. Both haunting and beautiful.

"Trapped inside these walls is where you reside, but there is another path that leads to the outside."

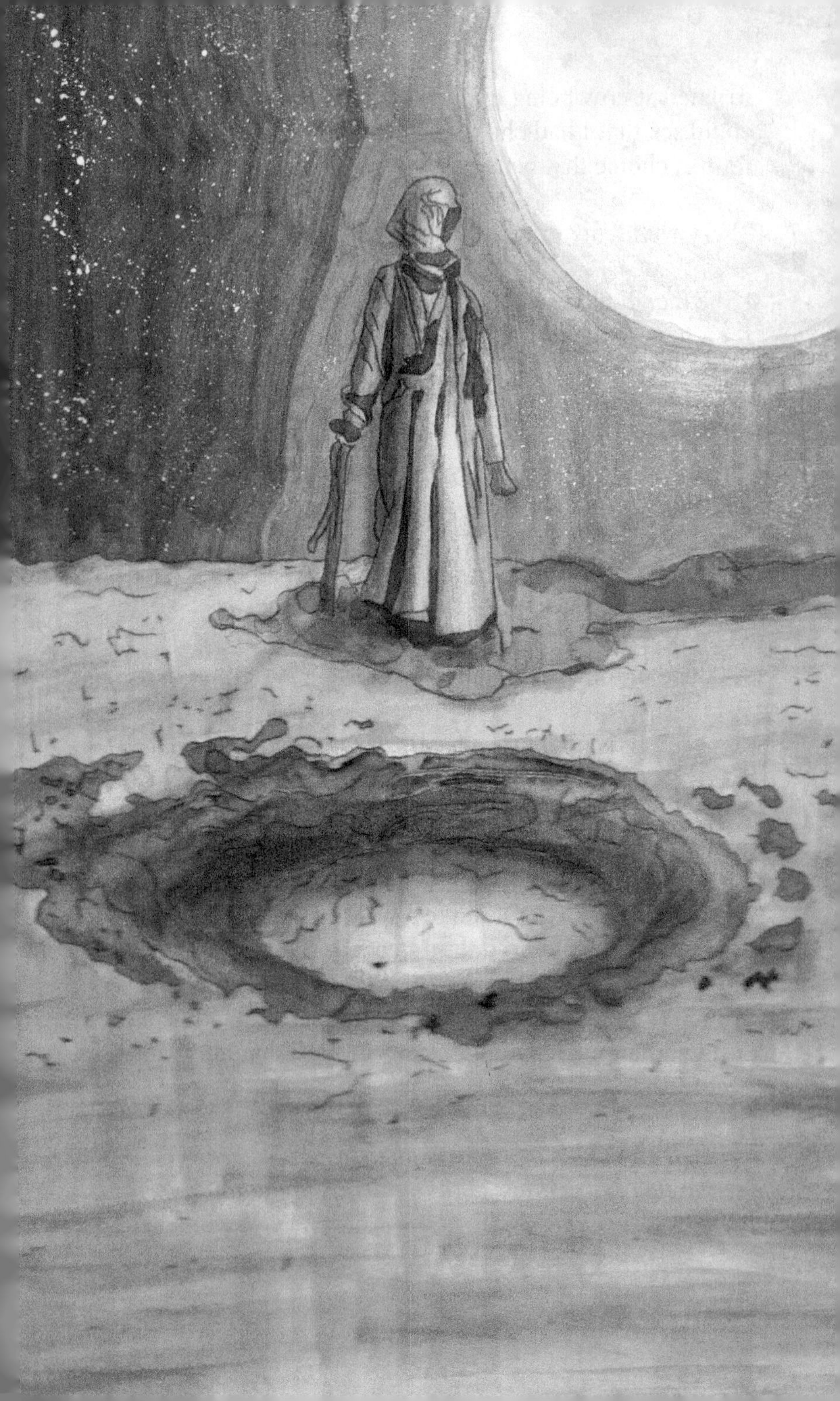

~ Chapter Nine: Mr. Star ~

"Who are you?" my grandmother asked the hooded stranger.

*"I am the prophet of all that could be,
within the bounds of all that you cannot see,"* whispered the stranger.

"Oh my!" Bonbon said excitedly. "I have heard of this fabled myth before. My mother told me all about it when I was a seedling. This is what's known as a dying star within our realm. A being capable of infinite magic."

"A dying star?" I asked.

"Yes. In our world, the night sky is lit up by immensely powerful beings with magical powers. When it is their time to die, they use their last bit of energy to grant wishes untold. They are forever rare and *very* desired."

"Wishes untold? You mean like a genie?" I asked.

"I do not know who Gene is. But if they can grant wishes, then yes, *just like Gene*," said Bonbon.

"One of these dying stars must have found its way through the rift," said my grandmother.

A conjurer of wishes was now in our presence. An opportunity and calling that we could not be guilty of ignoring. Though my voice was sparse, my intentions were pure. And after the journey I had been on, I knew I was now brave enough to command the stars.

"Mr. Star!" I yelled. "Might we respectfully ask you for a wish?'

*"My power is limitless, but also fading, while searching for regret.
I can only grant this wish to the one known as, Nicolette."*

"Me?! But why?!"

"From the time a star is born, they know exactly who will be the one to consume their last wish. It is predetermined from the moment of their birth," explained Bonbon.

I looked to my grandmother, our eyes meeting, and our thoughts plotting a course to the variety of wishes that I might ask for. Could I wish for us to be on the other side of this wall? Could I wish for my parents to be alive once more? Maybe I could wish for this horrible war to end. For things to go back to normal. For birds to fill the air once more with their glorious songs. How I missed their songs.

"Grandmother, what should I wish for?" I asked.

She simply smiled. A kind smile. A trusting smile that attached itself to my very heartbeat.

"That, my child, is up to you. Wishes are as rare as dying stars, and this one belongs to you."

"Mr. Star. Is there a limit to what you can do? Are you restricted by time or space? Or are your powers really that boundless?"

"I can shape mountains and move time within a whim, but there is still a journey and a sacrifice that you must face within."

"What kind of sacrifice?" my grandmother asked suspiciously.

*"A soul knows no bounds within the questions that are asked,
but her life may be lost if she does not complete the task."*

"What does that mean?!" asked Bonbon.

"I believe what they are saying, is that there will be great challenges to make this wish come true," my grandmother explained.

I thought about it for another moment. If Mr. Star could move time on a whim, then that was the only wish that mattered. I had it. A fool's dream.

"Mr. Star. I have made my decision," I announced.

*"Very well, tell me what your heart does desire.
I will grant it swiftly as if it were forged in fire."*

"I wish… that the rift had never arrived. That life and time had continued on as it used to be. That your world and ours had never met," I said.

*"This is a mighty wish, with rules that you must abide.
If you want it to happen, you will have to close the first rift from the other side."*

Then Mr. Star stepped back and a hole in the ground opened up. It extended deep into the darkness. Mysterious and frightening.

*"The path you must take resides through this shadowed gate.
You must leave behind all your promises and take this jump of faith."*

I peered down into the darkness. It made me nauseous just thinking about its unknown depths and what I might find deep below. Then I felt my grandmother and Bonbon both by my side. The three of us, ready for whatever path lay before us.

"Is this the rift?" I asked.

Bonbon laughed.

"No. No. This is just a hole in the ground. Not really sure where it goes. Believe me. When you see the rift, you will know. Your words will be reduced to a whisper by its beauty."

Deep breath. Time to be brave.

"Okay, Mr. Star. We are ready," I said.

*"The path that you are about to take, must be taken alone.
For the challenges that await you, are for you to face on your own."*

"No!" my grandmother yelled, pulling me away from the ledge and stepping in front of me. "I will go in her place. She is only a child!"

"She may be a child, but she has the strength of a storm. With only her bravery, she can return things to their original form."

We had been here before. My grandmother trying to sacrifice herself for me and my safety. But this had to be my journey now. There had to be a reason why I was the only one able to make this wish. Maybe it was all for naught. But if my destiny was to take me through the rift to turn back the clock, then I would meet that destiny with open arms.

"Grandmother," I said. "It's okay. I can do this. I have proven myself brave. This will simply be just another step in my journey. And at the end of it, we can be a family again. All of us. A real family."

My grandmother started to cry. She grabbed me and held me close to her.

"But what if you do not succeed? Or what if I lose you or you are hurt? Or... what if after you succeed, I am the same bitter woman that I was before? I don't want to be her. She was so angry. She was so foolish. And... she didn't have you in her life."

"No time for tears," I said softly.

I wiped the tears from my grandmother's cheek. My soft touch against her leathered and wrinkled skin.

"Because I will find you, and I will make sure that you have no choice but to let me into your life," I said.

"Do you promise?" she asked.

"I do. But now, you have to trust me and let me go."

"It's like you have grown up right before my very eyes on this journey, Nicolette. You are so very much like your mother."

I kissed my grandmother on her cheek and approached the mysterious hole in the ground. My toes peeked over its side, and my balance swayed back and forth as I prepared to fall into its shadowed embrace. I looked back towards my grandmother and Bonbon.

"Bonbon, thank you for all your help," I said.

"It has been my honor, Madam Nicolette."

"You got my name right!" I said with a laugh.

"Your name, little one, is one that is worth remembering," replied Bonbon.

"Nicolette?" asked my grandmother.

"Yes?"

"Tell your mother that I love her," she said as tears continued to fall from her aged eyes.

"I will tell her… and so will you. I'll see you soon," I whispered.

Then I closed my eyes, took a deep breath, and leaned forward, falling into the mysterious void.

*"Her journey, like a sunrise, has just now begun.
With hope and bravery, her wish will soon be won."*

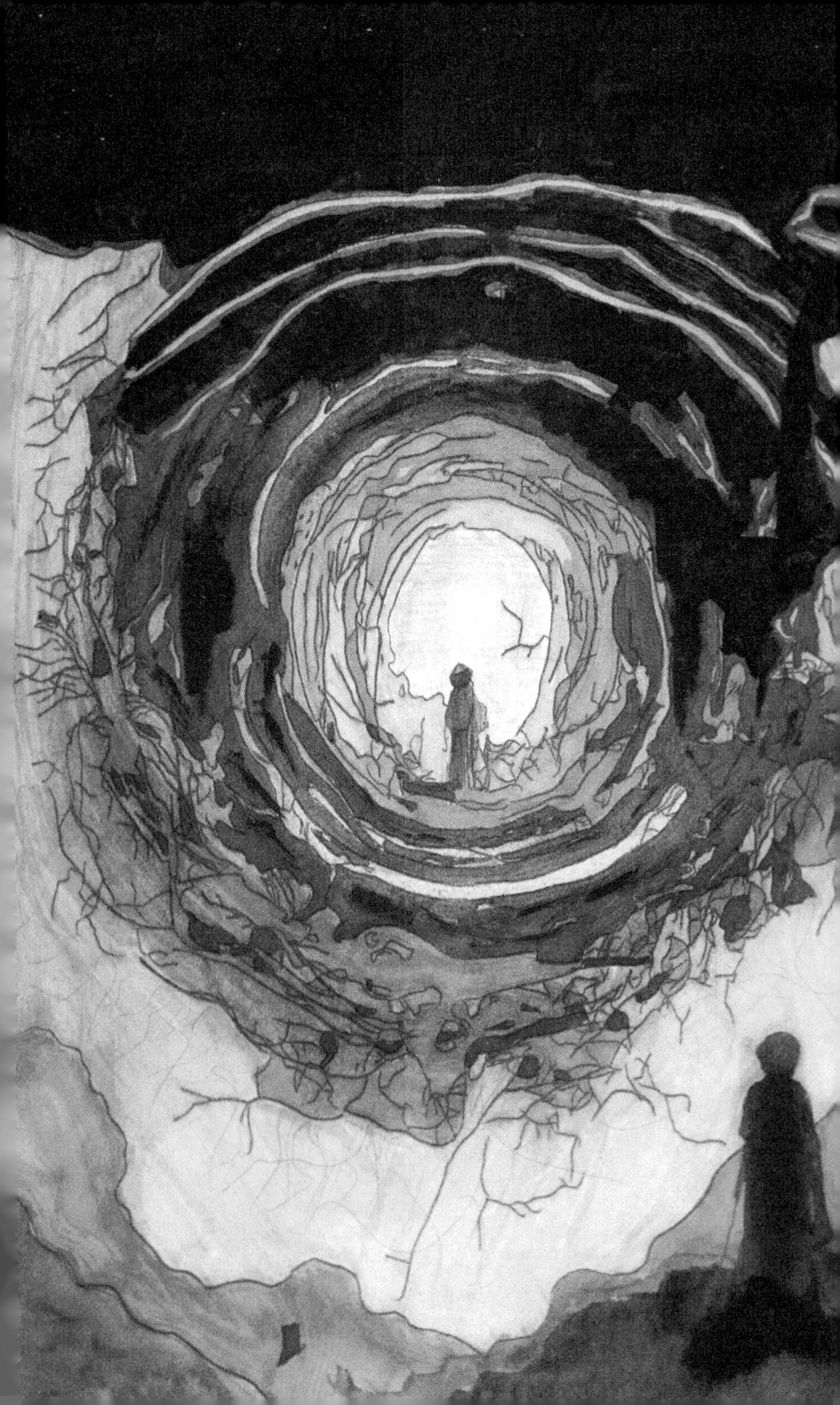

~ Chapter Ten: The Rift ~

Through that darkened void I found myself falling for the briefest of moments. As if suspended by a silent string, vibrating with the universe's rattle and hum. A modest song that sang of endless possibilities. But no sooner had I felt the sensation of falling, I was already where I was destined to be, being gently set down upon a soft surface. I opened my eyes to a world that was blurred and distorted. My fingers felt as if they had been submerged in static and snow, tingled, freezing, and pricked by a thorn from a rose. As my eyes adjusted, I found myself in what looked to be a cloud made up of multiple colors. They pulsed and shimmered as if each strand of light was singing its own song. Encroaching upon my soft ears was the sound of howling winds and beating hearts. Like the hearts of a whole other world were pounding at my consciousness.

Then to my right, I saw Mr. Star. The prophet of verse that had brought me here, wherever here was, and laid my path before me.

"Where am I?" I asked.

But Mr. Star did not reply, he only motioned my eyes towards the cloud suspended ahead of me, clutching to both the stars and ground in one motion. A swirling display of mystery that fell silent within this place of singing pulses and stirred echoes. An obvious doorway to the unknown. Bonbon was correct. My words were reduced to a whisper by this beauty.

"The rift," I whispered.

Mr. Star had transported me here to the rift's doorway. Moving my journey along across deserts and forests, leading me here. That darkened void was simply a shortcut to my destiny. A gateway that I now had no choice but to travel through. This was my purpose, and I had to accept that this was where I would either be destined to save worlds or die trying.

I started to approach this portal to the unknown. My hands trembled, with every step I took, drawing me closer to this mystery. These worlds and their vague future in my tiny shaking hands.

I turned back towards Mr. Star. But before I could say a word, there was a flash of light, almost blinding, and he vanished into thin air, leaving his cloak behind and an eerie hum buzzing throughout the wind's stale grip. An energy then filled the air. A presence, a mood. A lost voice that tiptoed across my arms and caused them to sprout goosebumps. I shivered. What was this feeling? A feeling as if I existed outside of time. As if the past had been washed away like bloodstained streets. A constant reminder that I was now in control of not only my own fate but the fate of two worlds. I felt all the energy of that dying star wrapped up in every breath that I now took. Pure power and energy within my heart and lungs, lacing my *very* soul with the supremacy of a massive sun.

I took a deep breath and pressed on. I had to find my courage. I had to see this through until the end, whatever that might be. I stepped into the rift. There was a small moment of calm before the rift grabbed hold of me and flung me across everything that had ever been. My arms and legs felt as if they were being stretched and skewed across the cosmos throughout all of time and space. I was one with everything and yet completely alone, all at once. The winds howled and screamed as the pulsing lights shouted, filling the air like an angry army. Chaos and flame, calmness, and water. All of it at one time until, eventually, everything just went dark.

But this was not the type of darkness we all experience when sleeping peacefully. No, this was like being trapped inside a void of nothingness, suspended by the universe like a marionette, and then being asked to dance for the heavens. But darkness does not always equal silence.

I could hear my mother now. It felt like she was near. Like I was being awakened from a deep sleep by her soft voice singing to me. A soft voice that was no louder than a whisper, rising to a heavenly crescendo. Words that I knew well. A song that she would sing to me every morning, forcing me to open my eyes, and greet every new day. Even within the walls of war, she still tried to raise my spirits at every dawn. Like the song of an army ready to do battle, even when marching into hopeless and mysterious places. This was a song that would guide even the most jaded soldier's bitter step.

Rise with the East my dreaming child.
With sunken sleepy eyes, we rise again.
In stepping like a drum, we rise again.
Let the day greet you with the boundless.
Let the day greet you with the endless.
Never more will we toss and turn.
For if we rise with the East, we are forever grateful.

Her breath still lingered behind every single word, leaving chills upon my restless neck. Was I sleeping? Was I dreaming? Did I dare to know what path lay before me? Covered with memories and ghosts that were both restless and comforting.

I could then hear my father and his gruff laugh. It was boisterous and ageless, practically shaking the walls of our house. He was a large man, who worked long days. But no matter what, he would always make the effort to chase me around the house or play whatever foolish game I wanted. No matter how tired he was. No matter how much horror and frustration he had seen on that day. No matter how much death he had held. He still made time to find laughter and be a loving father. He dared not rob me of my childish nature, even within a damaged world.

Suddenly, a long-lost memory made its way into my thoughts. A memory of when I had found a weathered portrait of my grandmother. A painting of her and my mother from when my mother was about my age. My grandmother looked stern and stoic in this painting. Statue-like in all her nature, with her famous scowl captured perfectly. She was young. Her hand placed upon my mother's shoulder. My mother had never known her father, as he had died when she was quite young. So, it was just the two of them. Alone. No one else to keep them company or make them feel loved. My mother's face was… well… sad. That was the only way I could think to describe it. Sadness.

After finding it, I had asked my mother about the painting. She stood there in shock, as if I had uncovered something she'd thought was long forgotten. Then, without a single word, she grabbed it from me, threw it out in the garbage, and then immediately hugged me. She sobbed as she held me close. All of her regrets and broken hearts singing loudly with every tear. To know how my mother must have suffered when she was growing up. Not knowing the love of one's own mother. A loss that can break souls. And then, for my grandmother to stop speaking to her altogether once my mother had found the love of her life. It was surely heartbreaking. I remembered telling my mother that everything was going to be okay. At my frail age, comforting her as she cried. If only she could have seen the woman that my grandmother had turned into after the rift had arrived. A kind soul, with a secret. Painted in regrets, thick as honey. Longing for a past where she could have found a brighter future.

If I was to be successful in my quest to turn back time, would my mother still harbor those same feelings? Would my grandmother even open that door to us?

I then felt a strong wind splashing at my face, tickling my cheeks, and prodding at my ears. Falling, falling in darkness. Then the feeling of the ground fast approaching. Panic set in and I opened my mouth to scream. Silent screams were all that could be heard though. For no matter how hard I tried, I could no more scream than whisper, and no more whisper than scream. I was silent. With the wind washing against my body, falling in silence with the ground fast approaching, reality itself turned into no more than a mystery and a story. One in which I played the lead of this tragic affair.

The next thing I knew, I found myself in a vast field. A field that looked to be filled with something resembling wheat. Golden, swaying in the soft breeze, side to side. I looked to the sky and was left speechless. The heavens carried three moons, and the stars darted around, bouncing off of the sky's existence. In hues of green and purple, these skies were not like the skies of my world. No, I was somewhere new. Somewhere foreign. I was now on the other side of the rift. A world never before seen by mine. I had arrived.

In the distance, I heard a mighty roar. A roar that begged me to run away from it. But my steadied step chose instead to press forward. Against all doubt that I carried within, that roar moved my step directly towards it. I had been drawn here to face whatever was needed to close the rift. And something told me, that roar was where I was destined to go. As I made my way through these endless wheat fields, towards certain danger, I happened upon what looked to be a scarecrow. Massive in size, it towered over me, casting a shadow across my brow. It was dressed in some kind of military garb and wore a hollowed-out stone on its head like a hat.

"Greetings, my strange friend," I said with a slight giggle.

Suddenly, as if awakened by my voice, the wheat of the fields fluttered and shook. For what I had thought were plants, gently swaying in the breeze, were actually a swarm of flying creatures, resembling golden locusts. The stocks of these plants opened and began to flap wildly before leaping towards the heavens, disappearing to the skies, leaving me in an empty field, with only this peculiar scarecrow by my side.

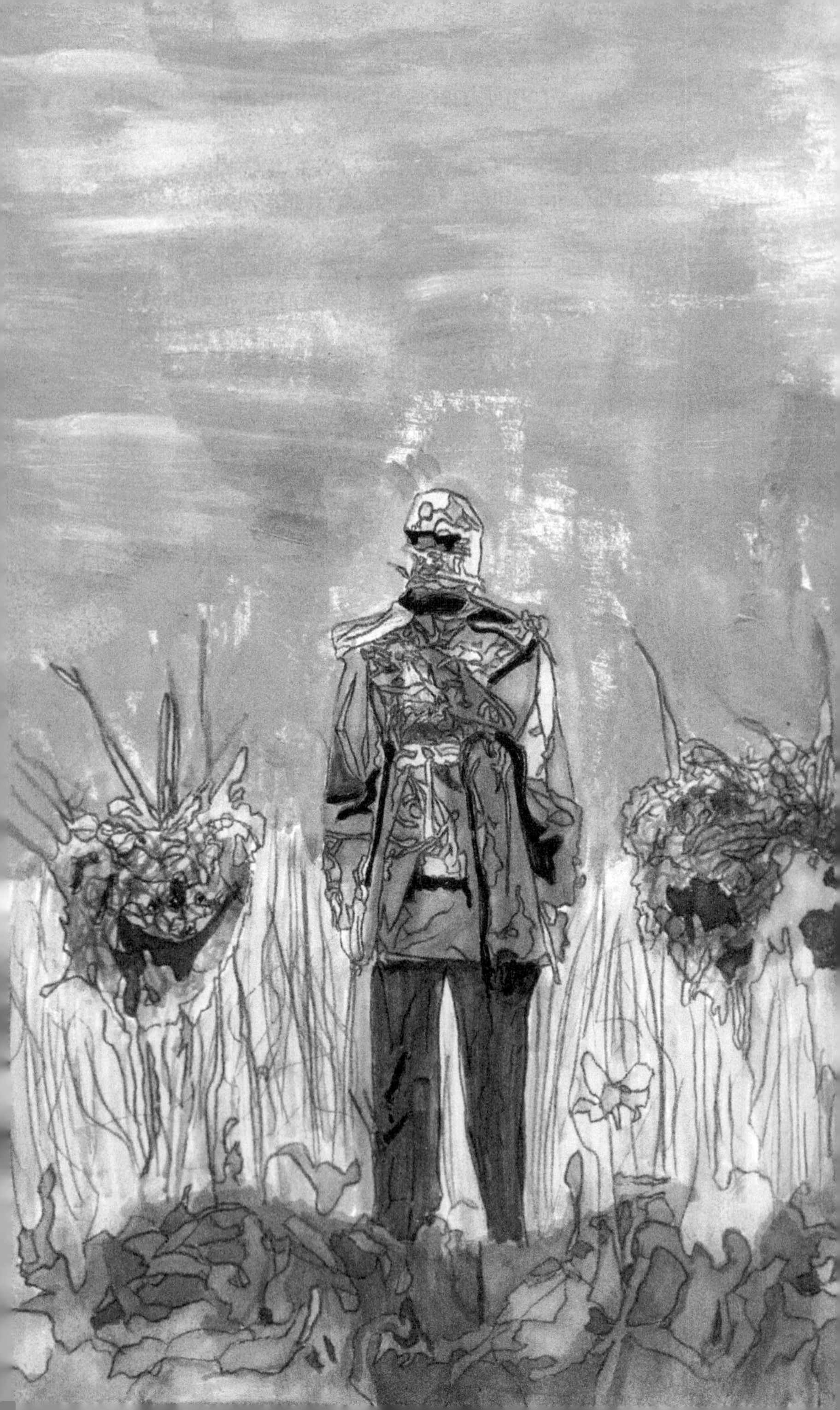

~ Chapter Eleven: The Great General ~

After I had caught my breath, I looked at my lifeless friend.

"Looks like it's just you and me now," I said, before turning away and pressing on with my journey, towards the ominous roar over the horizon.

Then I heard a rustle come from the scarecrow. I turned my head just in time to catch the scarecrow's head moving on its own and looking directly at me. I stopped in my tracks, unsure if I was just imagining things.

"Hello?" I said, greeting the inanimate object with caution.

The scarecrow then stretched like it was waking up on an early morning before starting to move towards me. It slowly stomped and stumbled as if it had not taken a step in an exceptionally long time. It sort of looked like a monster with the way that it walked and lunged at me. I was not sure if I should run or stand true to the ground beneath me. But so far, these creatures had been nothing but kind to my cause.

"Is your name, by chance, Nicolette?" the strange creature asked me in a low gravelly voice.

How did this creature know my name?

"Why yes, I am. But to be honest, I'm not sure how you know my name. Not to mention the fact that I am surprised to hear a creature from this side of the rift pronounce it correctly."

"Well, I have been waiting an *awfully* long time for you to arrive. So, I have committed your name to memory."

"You've been waiting for me? But why?!"

"That is a very long story," the scarecrow laughed.

"Okay… But it does seem like a story that I might need to know before pressing on with my journey. Wouldn't you agree?" I replied.

"Oh, yes. How silly of me."

The scarecrow cleared his throat, preparing to explain all that I needed to know.

"When the rift opened, I volunteered to take control of our armies and lead the charge against this new threat. We were always a peaceful society, so we had no real history of war or violence. But soon, the war consumed me. Consumed all of us. And eventually, with so much death, I just wanted the sun to set, and this all to end. We were fighting an unwinnable battle. So, I searched for a dying star, and after much looking, I finally found one. Once I did, I wished for the rift to have never opened. My wish was supposedly granted, but the star instructed me to first stand in this field, still as the ground, and wait for the one who called herself Nicolette. Only then would my wish be made true."

"See, that story was not too long," I said.

"Well, to be fair, I did have a *very* long time to rehearse it."

Was this my destiny? To team up with this great general and change the course of history for both of our worlds?

"I also met a dying star and made the same wish as you. I am surprised that you speak my language though. I thought that only within the garden walls could we understand each other."

"I know not about a great wall. But wishes made on stars transcend all languages and words. Meaning, your words will be heard by all, as will mine. As long as they are needed for the journey and fate."

"So, I guess we will be on this journey together then?" I asked.

"The star told me that I would guide you to the mouth of the beast and that once there, you would defeat it."

"What beast? The source of the roar that I have been hearing?"

"Yes. Let me show you, Nicolette."

Across these empty fields, we traveled. I followed close behind the great general, putting my faith in him and his direction. I had tried to ask his name, but no matter the power of shooting stars, I could still not understand the seemingly random collection of screeching and moaning that had erupted from his mouth. So, for now, I would simply call him, *the great general*. For according to him, that is what he was. Eventually, we walked up a soft hill and then peered down into a mighty valley. Within this valley was a city. A city as big as any I had ever seen within my world. Tall buildings and small shops. Houses where perhaps more strange creatures lived. Everything seemed to be made of plants. Wrapped in vines and soaked in dirt. A world that was alive.

On the horizon, I caught a glimpse of what was making that terrible roar. Something as big as an ocean and as fierce as a storm. A force that had haunted my nightmares for what felt like forever. Something that had taken everything from me and left me devastated within its ruin. It was The Red Sea. Except, it now wore the hue of green like a king's robe. Monstrous and alive, far off in the distance. It loomed over this place the same way that it did in ours, menacing and deadly. Why was it trying to destroy its own world? Could it be that this harbinger of death was just as poisonous within this side of the rift as it was on ours?

"That is the beast that you must defeat," revealed the great general.

"But how?" I asked.

"I… do not know."

I did not find this very reassuring. If whole armies on my side could not manage to defeat The Red Death, then what hope did I have?

We made our way into the city. As we approached, I started to notice that many of these plants were dead or dying. Whole trees and buildings that had been toppled over and left to rot under these three moons and this world's purple hue. This land had been ravaged with the same vile touch as ours. It was ripe with devastation and loss. Where our streets ran red with blood, this place was covered with the aroma of rotting plants, ripped and shredded, left to die on the vine. It was hard to tell which of these once-blooming corpses were simply structures and which were the creatures that made up this land. Perhaps both were true.

Once in this city of plants, I noticed how lifeless it truly was. It was as if this place had been abandoned.

"Hello?!" I yelled.

My voice echoed throughout the empty streets, bouncing off of root and vine. I waited for a reply, but none came. Where were the voices of the survivors?

"Is there anyone left besides yourself?" I asked the general.

"There is, we just have to draw them out. They are *very* scared to make themselves known."

Then the general erupted into a howling song that filled the air. A song that reminded me of the melody brought forth by the Elders that had guided the way to my grandmother. After the song had faded into soft decay, a tiny flower sprouted up from the ground in front of us and blossomed into a child. A child made of petals and twigs. They stared up at me, with eyes made of raindrops, and a smile that seemed to bloom. Surely seeing a human here was shocking to the creatures of this world.

"Hello. I don't mean to alarm you," I said softly. "I know I must look very strange to you. My name is Nicolette, and I am from the other side of the rift."

The child looked at me curiously, up, and down, then glanced over at the great general.

"It is not what you look like, but why you are here that they care about," said the great general.

"Who are you?" asked an unseen voice.

I turned around to find myself, and the great general, attracting the curiosity of a slowly growing crowd. Creatures that were the same type as Bonbon and Fonfroo. But even stranger and more varied. With shapes and configurations so abstract that they could live on museum walls.

One of the creatures, who was almost squid-like, with tentacles and no eyes, gradually floated over to me, suspended in the air like it was surrounded by water.

"I said, who are you?" the creature asked again.

"I, um, my name is Nicolette," I replied.

The creatures all gasped in unison.

"That is not a name that we are familiar with," said the still-hovering creature.

"What kind of name is Nancy?" yelled one of the creatures.

"I don't know! But you are right. Nelly is a very odd name!" yelled another one of the creatures.

At this point in my journey, I had given up all hope of my name being pronounced correctly by the masses. As long as the first letter was there, then I would consider the conversation a rousing success.

"I am not from here. I am from the other side of the rift," I revealed.

The creatures, once again, all gasped in unison.

"Then it is your kind that has brought death upon our land!" yelled one of the creatures.

"It was not me!" I argued.

Why were they blaming me for the beast that they had released into our world? Maybe something about the rift had angered it and caused it to manifest such devastation.

"Lies! If you are from the other side, then you have done nothing but try and destroy us!" screamed another creature.

"I promise! I can explain!" I yelled.

The crowd grew louder and uglier, slowly converging upon us. Ready to blame me for all of the misfortunes that had befallen them. If only they would listen to me. If only they would understand that we had been destroyed and hunted by the same monster as themselves.

"Let this strange visitor speak!" yelled the great general.

The great general had calmed the crowd, pleading with them to just let me be heard. I had been given a voice to share my story with a crowd that desired nothing but revenge. So not a word could be wasted. The mob of creatures went silent, standing on the edge, waiting to hear what I had to say.

"I am from the other side of the rift. I have traveled here by means of a dying star that found its way to my world."

"A dying star?! That is astronomically rare!" yelled one of the creatures.

"So, I have been told," I replied. "But my only purpose for being here is to help seal the rift and make it like our two worlds never collided. All that I ask, is that you call back your beast. The one that we call The Red Sea."

"What is *The Red Sea*?" asked the great general.

"Why, the beast that you said I must face. The beast that lies just beyond the horizon. The beast that stands as tall as a mountain. One of these creatures escaped from your world to mine and is killing a great many of us!"

"But, that creature, the one of which you speak, is not from our world. It's from yours," he revealed.

"What do you mean?!"

"The creature that you call The Red Sea did not come from here. It attacked us, appearing from the rift, and starting this war against us. It is the only thing we know of your world. For nothing else has come through."

"But did you not all open the portal?"

"No. It was the beast that opened the portal. It crashed through, and then, soon after, began consuming us."

"I don't understand…"

"We will show you," said the great general.

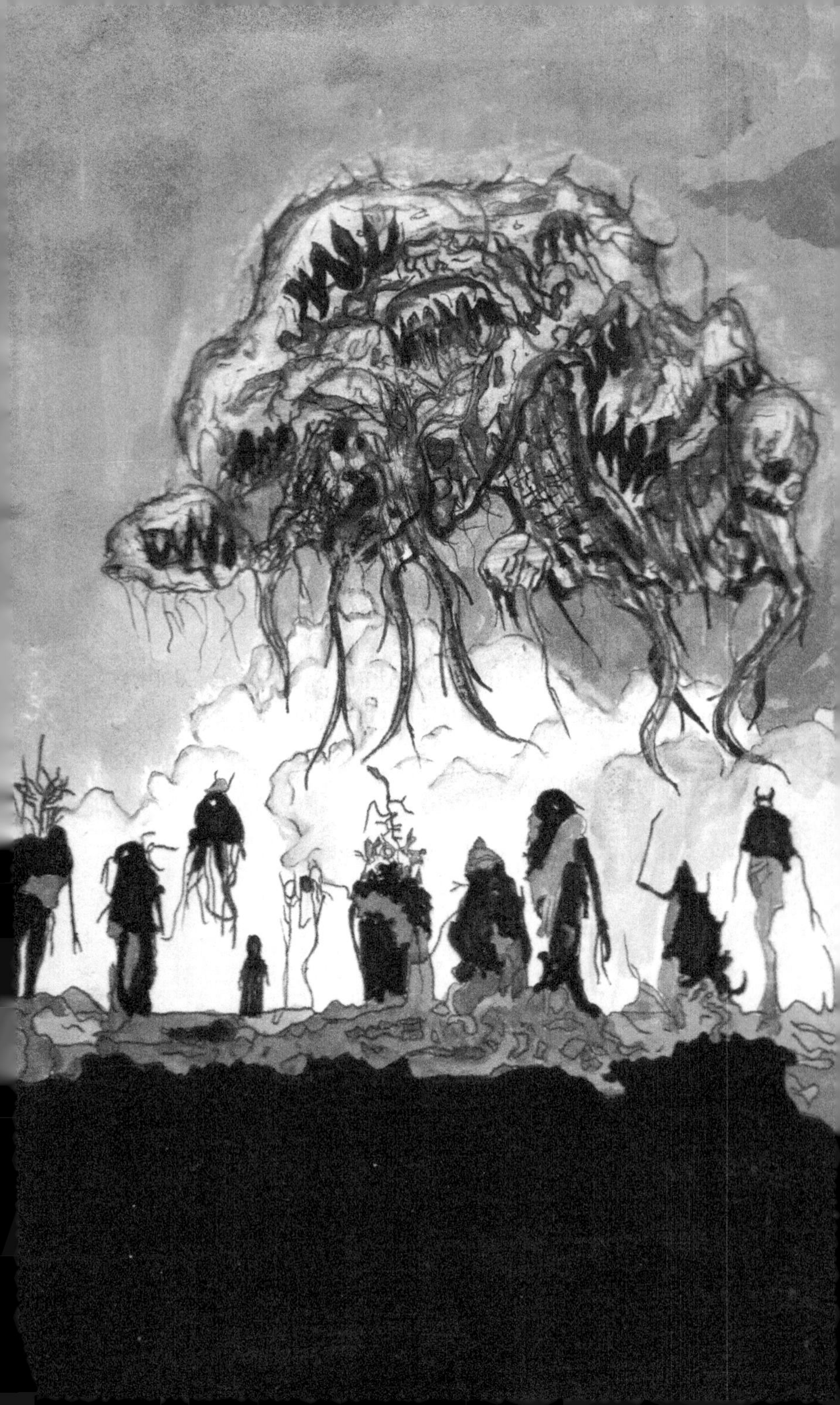

~ Chapter Twelve: In War & Sorrow ~

"Many zoolooz ago..." started the great general.

"Wait... what is a zoolooz?" I asked.

"Um... Well, it is one rotation around our mighty star!"

"We call them years."

"What?"

"Years. That's what we call them on my world. Can you just call them years? Zoolooz sounds silly and makes me giggle," I explained.

"Fine. Many *years* ago... we lived in great peace. We never fought. We never judged. We lived in what could be considered near perfection."

The great general then led me to the edge of their city to a clearing where the ground was scarred with ash. It was the size of a city block, with nothing left alive. No specs of green or purple touched this place of death. And in the middle of this desolate space, spinning in colors and sound, was their side of the rift. Open and waiting for whatever to travel right through it and into our world.

"And then one day, the rift opened and released a monstrous beast made of metal and fire into our world. When it crashed, it brought with it a massive explosion that shook the cities and scorched the ground, leaving behind this ash-covered wasteland."

I stepped inside this patch of decay, away from life, with only death beneath my step, and made my way towards a pile of twisted metal that lay to the side of the rift. It was still somehow smoldering from when it had arrived, like an eternal flame. As I approached, I saw writing on the side of it. It was in my language.

"Test 1-7 atomic antimatter projectile," I read aloud.

My heart sank. I had heard my parents talk about such weapons before. Dangerous science experiments that could stretch and skew the very fabric of reality and time. Dreamt up by wicked men to be used in the name of power and war.

"What… what happened after it exploded?" I asked.

"It killed many of us, and then after the fires had settled, within the clouds of smoke, it released two monsters. One of which returned through the rift, and the other which has remained here, traveling our world, consuming all within its path, and glowing green with the blood of those whom we love."

The Red and Green Seas were our doing. My world's. A product of the selfish and tyrannical trying to gain power and harness the sun. The frozen forest was known by many as a place that few lived or went to. What had the leaders of our world been creating out there? Assessing their sharpened teeth on the jaws of war and destruction.

The blood of others being their compass and setting sun. Power. Power over mortality. That had been the arrow that pierced the universe and created the rift.

"So, it is *our* fault. All of this," I whispered.

The great general sensed my sadness and placed his root-encrusted hand on my shoulder to try and comfort me.

"This is not your fault. I am no fool. I'll assume that this travesty was unleashed by a mere handful of evil souls," said the great general.

"But still. It came from us. Not from you. You were peaceful before this."

"We still had evil before the rift. Not much, but some. There was one known as Erra, who was the evilest criminal in our lands. But then he disappeared, escaping through the second rift to bring his clever devastation upon your world. And that… that was our responsibility. That was our fault."

"I met Erra. I helped to vanquish him," I said proudly.

"Ah, then you are already braver than most."

"Wait… the second rift."

I had almost forgotten about the mysterious rift that had brought me to this strange land. A destined path with an unknown origin. Had we also created that? Why was it there?

"Where did the second rift come from? The one in which Erra escaped and I traveled?" I asked.

"When I met the dying star and made my wish, they opened that doorway for you to come through. That is why I was waiting there for you. I waited for many a zooloo… er… I mean, year."

"So, then, the second rift was meant for me all along?"

"Always. It was always your destiny to walk through that doorway."

"Then everything that has happened to me. My parents dying. Meeting my grandmother. Following her into the garden. Her being captured. My journey. Her rescue. All of it… it was always meant to be?" I asked.

"As sure as wishing on a dying star."

I felt angry. What kind of strange, sick game was the universe trying to play on me? The suffering of two worlds. The killing of so many. All of this, just to turn back the hands of time. To make it as if none of this had ever happened.

"But then, what was the point of any of this? What was the point in breaking my heart?! In killing millions?!" I asked as tears streamed down my face.

The great general paused for a moment. He collected his thoughts and breathed deeply, looking to the sky, ready to bestow his greatest of wisdom on my blistered thoughts.

"I do not know," he finally said.

Maybe it is not the responsibility of those in charge to imbue great meaning behind mysterious happenings. After all, it was the leaders of *my* world that had caused this whole mess.

"All of this death and disaster. And it is now up to me to fix everything? It hardly seems like a wish come true. I do not even know what to do," I said.

"Perhaps if we find the beast, then once you are there, fate will take over and you will know what to do," suggested the great general.

"Maybe. But I am so frightened of it. What could a child like me possibly do against The Green Sea?!"

"Dying stars have never been known to send anyone in the wrong direction. Every plan has a meaning. Every wish has an outcome. It will come to you. After all, I thought that I would just grow old and die in that field where I was waiting for you. But then, there you came, arriving just as had been predicted."

This made me feel slightly better. I stared off into the distance, The Green Sea almost within my grasp. It had to be now. I had to face my fears. No more stalling. No more excuses. My destiny was to save two worlds with no weapons against a monster that stood a mile high. I had to trust Mr. Star. I had to trust my chosen path.

"Will there only be you at my side?" I asked the great general.

He chuckled and motioned behind us where a small crowd had begun to form. They were all prepared to stand by my side as we journeyed towards our destinies and marched into battle. Interlocked by our shared thirst to turn back the hands of time and lead us to a brighter alternate future.

"I believe that there are still many of us who carry faith in the power of a dying star and the wish of a stranger," he said.

And so, we marched on. A small army, against the backdrop of almost certain death. I had no idea what I could do. But I stood tall and moved onward, all while humming a soft tune in my head.

> *Rise with the East my dreaming child.*
> *With sunken sleepy eyes, we rise again.*
> *In stepping like a drum, we rise again.*
> *Let the day greet you with the boundless.*
> *Let the day greet you with the endless.*
> *Never more will we toss and turn.*
> *For if we rise with the East, we are forever grateful.*

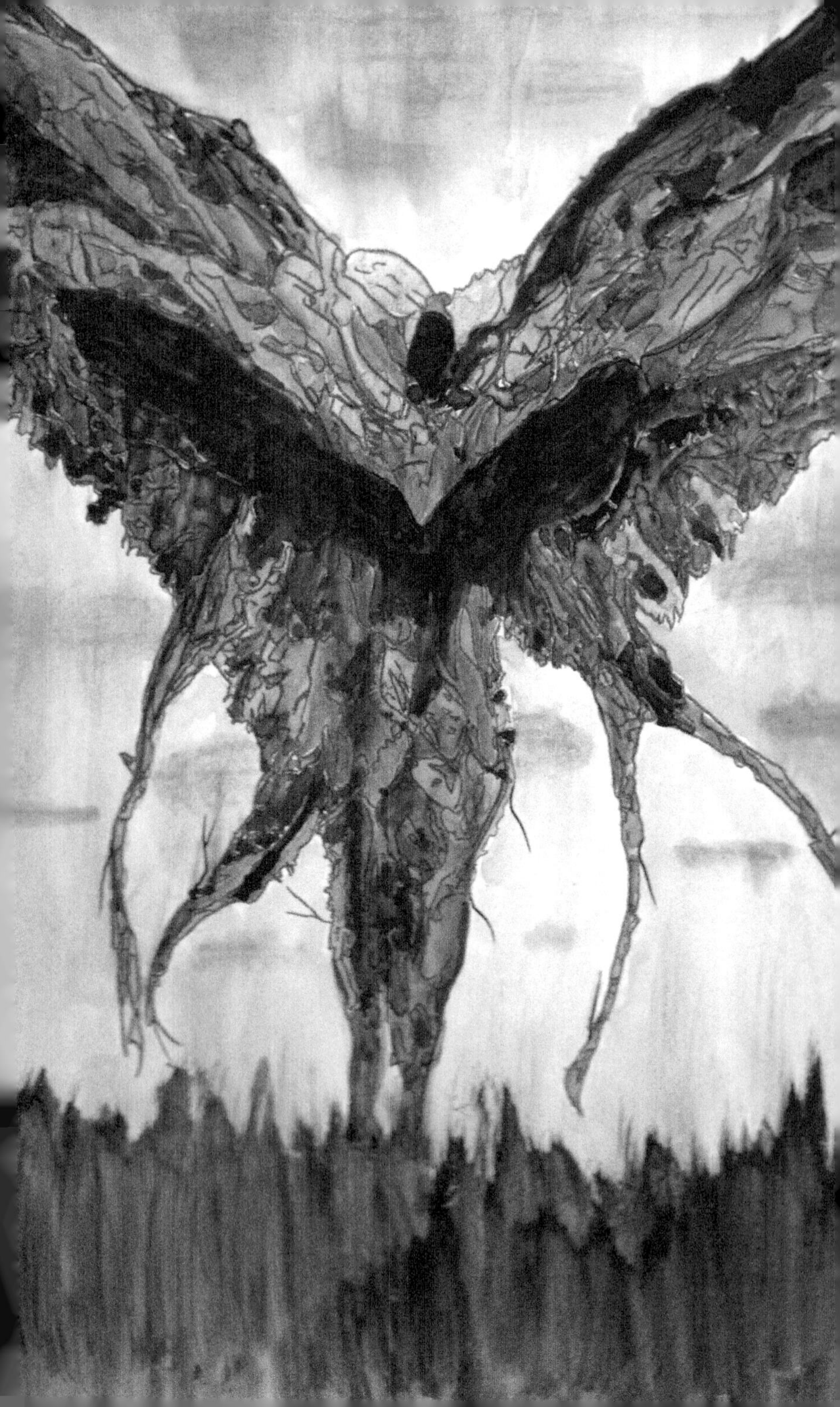

~ Chapter Thirteen: The Green Sea ~

War is something that cannot be explained. It can only be felt, observed, and lived. But nothing, no manner of story or fear, can prepare you for the chaos surrounding it. The subtle growl from each swing of the blade, like a rabid wolf desperate to devour at random and satisfy its hunger.

As we approached The Green Sea, it became clear that it could sense our presence. The skies were blocked out by the beast and the ground shook with no reprieve as this monster roared at my tiny army. It was a predator, and it smelled fresh meat. Maybe it specifically sensed me, something new, made of flesh and bone instead of leaf and root. The sky lit up in shades of darkened greens and reds as lightning and thunder filled the air, clogging my lungs with a feeling of dread.

Suddenly, from deep beneath the ground, tentacles sprouted that were made of clouds. The arms of this beast, sent forward to protect itself from me. Maybe The Green Sea knew that I was more of a threat than even I realized. The tentacles shot at me and the small army, piercing one of the creatures in the chest that stood to my left. They shrieked with pain and then immediately disintegrated. A life lost in a split second, their *very* being reduced to no more than dust.

"NO!" I screamed.

With mourning eyes, I turned to look at the army that stood bravely at my side. I did not want to see any more of them suffer or die. My kind had already brought enough death to this world, and I did not want to be responsible for any more loss.

"You all need to turn back! Now! I cannot see anyone else die!" I ordered.

The great general made his way to my side, just as a tentacle erupted from the ground, heading right towards us. Without warning, the general sprouted mighty spikes from his forearm and swatted at the tentacle, cutting it in half and turning it into a small pile of ashes.

"We will not leave your side. For if you succeed, then all of those who have died will live again!" he yelled.

"No! I cannot be the one that leads you to your deaths!" I argued.

I had spent many years in the company of death, and I no longer wanted to be in its presence.

"Nicolette! We are going to fight this war *with* or *without* your blessing. The question is…are you brave enough to lead us?!"

I stared into the distance at The Green Sea. It was close now. So close that I could feel it staring back at me. It was as if our eyes were locked in an eternal battle. But through this connection, I could feel its fear, even though it tried to hide it deep below. I could also see its weakness. It was curious about me. It wanted to understand why I was different from the rest of this world. It was also prideful. Maybe I could use that to my advantage.

"Very well," I finally replied. "But I just need to get close enough to touch the beast. I don't know why. But I can feel it. It is scared of me and my touch. But I am also a mystery that it longs to solve. So, just get me close, and then I want you all to retreat!"

"Alright lads!" yelled the great general. "You heard her! We protect Nicolette at all costs! Charge!"

The small army ran beside me as we swiftly made our way towards what most would consider certain death. But we were fearless, and all just screamed in the face of this danger, approaching the wall of clouds that had transformed into sharpened spikes before our path. It seemed to almost gallop towards us, screaming and hissing. The weaponized arms of The Green Sea, coming to slaughter us all.

Suddenly, the army beside me all morphed, transforming their limbs into weapons, and cutting down this cloud army that was trying to block them. They cleared my path before I could even travel it. Faster and faster, I ran. I ran towards the heart of the beast. I could hear it thumping from deep within. A saddened and angry song that called out to me. Gone was my fear. No more was I worried. My feet led me in the direction of my victory. For my world, for theirs, for my mother and father, for *every* lost life that now had the chance to breathe again.

With every step forward, I could hear my army dying, dissolving into nothing. I so badly wanted to collapse to the ground and mourn every single one of them. I so badly wanted to just sob and scream with every life that this monster took. But I held back my tears and pressed on. One foot in front of the other.

"No time for tears!" I screamed.

As I neared The Green Sea, its shadow cascaded down over me, completely blocking out the sky and turning my world into total darkness. I ran at it. What was I going to do? I peeked back over my shoulder, just in time to see the great general be killed by the beast. His last words rang through the air.

"Victory is within your grasp!!!" he screamed before being turned to dust.

I ran as fast as my legs would carry me, as the tentacles of this beast chased me, nipping at my heels but still not being able to catch me. Finally, I found myself about to run into the beast. I held my breath, closed my eyes, and fell into the cloud before me, immediately finding myself in a silent fog that stole my step and left me only hearing the beating of a heart. Before I could catch my breath, a voice filled the air.

"WHAT ARE YOU?!" it screamed.

Its voice was louder than any ocean, shaking the ground while proudly wearing the title of *predator*. I could smell the stench of rotting plants dripping from the inside of this beast. Its walls covered in the blood of this world. I imagined what horror I would see and feel if I had been trapped inside the beast from my side. The smell of copper and a scarlet hue that would linger in the fine air. It would be a nightmare of infinite terror.

"My name is Nicolette!" I replied.

"HMMM. YOU ARE, FAMILIAR TO ME. NOT FROM THIS WORLD, BUT FROM ANOTHER. ANOTHER WORLD. ONE IN WHICH I WAS BIRTHED. A COLLECTION OF SCIENCE AND CHEMICALS, TEARING A HOLE BETWEEN THESE REALMS AND BEING BORN INTO GREATNESS. AND NOW I HUNGER. I HUNGER ALL THE TIME. MY SIBLING HUNGERS FOR BLOOD, WHILE I HUNGER FOR VINES. TO LIVE OFF WHATEVER LAND WE OCCUPY AND DESTROY WHATEVER TRIES TO STOP US. FOR WE ARE GREATNESS. BEINGS WORTHY OF WORSHIP."

"Well, then you won't like me very much!"

"AND WHY IS THAT?!"

"Because I'm here to destroy you!"

"AND JUST HOW EXACTLY DO YOU PLAN ON DOING THAT, CHILD?!"

The belly of The Green Sea then erupted with lightning and thunder, crashing all around me, barely missing my step. I stood tall though, ready to fight. Somehow. Someway.

"I AM THE DEFINITION OF PERFECTION, YOU SIMPLE, STUPID, CHILD. YOU ARE AN INSECT, AND I AM THE SUN!"

Pride, it seemed, would play the role of a blade in this story. It was the confidence of my world and thirst for power that had first brought this beast to life. It would have to be the beast's own ego that would bring it down and collapse it in upon itself. I knew what had to be done. I would admire the beast, which was something it obviously craved.

"You seem *very* self-assured. You must have great strength!"

"I DO! I AM MORE POWERFUL THAN THE UNIVERSE!"

"I see, well then, you must be very smart as well!"

"I AM! SMARTER THAN ANY AND ALL WHO HAVE EVER THOUGHT A THOUGHT BEFORE NOW!"

"Hmmmm. Well, if you are as strong and smart as you say, you must be powered by a mighty heart!"

"I AM! IT IS MIGHTIER THAN A RAGING STORM!"

"Then it must be very impressive to see!"

"IT IS!"

"Well then, clearly, I am no match for you! I was a great fool to ever think that I could defeat such an infinite power! Might I ask you one request though?!"

The beast just laughed.

"WHAT COULD YOU POSSIBLY WANT WHILE STARING DOWN THE FANGS OF YOUR OWN DEATH?!"

"Before you eat me! Might I have one look at your heart?! I would love to be in awe of its great power and spend my last moments worshiping it!"

"AH! YES! YOU MAY WORSHIP IT!"

Without any hesitation, The Green Sea slowly released an orb from high within itself, hovering from above. It glowed like fire, red and pulsating. The power that set this beast apart from all others. The beast lowered its heart further and further until it was just above my head.

"DO YOU SEE?! DO YOU SEE TRUE POWER?!" The Green Sea asked.

"I do! But… might I get an even closer look?!"

"VERY WELL! BUT THEN I WILL DEVOUR YOU!"

"Sounds like a marvelous plan," I said with a smile.

The Green Sea lowered its heart even more until it was just in front of me. And then, before it could react, I ripped the aigrette from my hair and stabbed the beast in the heart, using all my strength. Made by my mother. Given to me by my grandmother. Destined to be my sword. Their power and voices by my side. All three souls clutching the hairpiece and vanquishing this evil. A destiny filled with loss, but one that was always meant to be. The strength of three generations, estranged, and living in regrets, coming together to save two worlds. Like three warriors driving a blade into death itself.

   The monster screamed and shook, beginning to crumble and die. I could see as it began to be torn apart, sending a mountain of ashes falling right towards me. Like the darkest of rainclouds destined to consume me. My vision started to go dark, and I took in one last deep breath before I was consumed by a victorious death over The Green Sea.

I had done it.

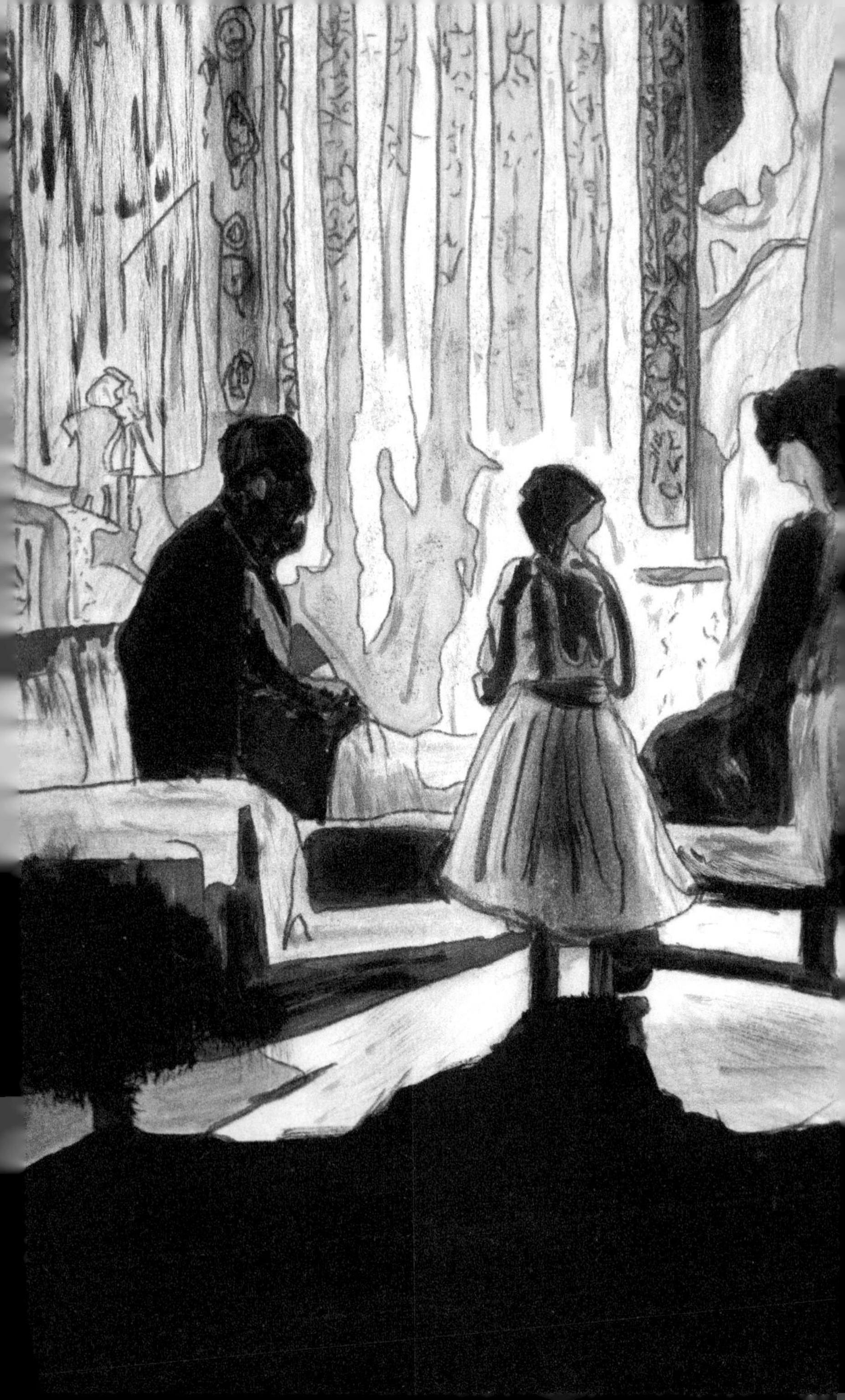

~ Chapter Fourteen: Time & Time Again ~

I was abruptly awakened, unexpectedly finding myself back home. Like a dream in which you are falling, faster and faster towards your own death. But then, at the last second, you are jolted awake just before hitting the ground. The morning air breathed through a nearby window as birdsongs filled the softened breeze. Wait, birds? What was happening? Was I dead? Was this heaven? My thoughts were clouded and slow to focus. Suddenly, it all came to me. Like a flash of blinding light, rushing through my body, and opening my eyes to reality.

I had two lives that now lived within my head. I could remember the last few years. The rift, the horror, The Red Sea, my parents living and dying, meeting my grandmother, endless gardens, devastating evils, dying stars, great generals, and the ultimate sacrifice. But at the same time, I could remember the last few years as if the rift had never happened. Happiness, birthdays, rainstorms, a broken wrist, a trip to the zoo, a new best friend, and the list went on and on, almost endlessly. Two lives, both living within my mind. One of tragedy and fear. The other of hope and love. All these moments and memories, now stitched together with a single thread. They had collided, leaving only the here and now. A single strand wrapped up inside a glorious tapestry.

I vaguely remembered my mother and father talking to each other, a few years ago, about a group of power-hungry men that were caught trying to test some kind of new weapon deep within the frozen forest.

"Who knows what might have happened if they had succeeded," said my mother.

"Thankfully they didn't," replied my father.

In this world, the one where I was currently crawling out of bed, there had never been a rift. I remembered waking up on that particular morning, the day when those power-hungry men had been stopped. As the sun rose, and filled the sky with soft warmth, life just seemed brighter. That day, as I walked with my parents to the park, I saw smiles in abundance everywhere I looked. They may not have remembered the world as I did. They may have all forgotten the horror and death that they had either survived or been lost to. But they all knew that something was different. That they had somehow been blessed with a second chance.

I stepped out of bed, onto the soft hand-sewn rug that was right next to me, slipping a pair of wool socks on my feet, and standing tall, stretching as if I was trying to reach for the stars.

I remembered several months ago, going to the store with my mother. Then there, as if by magic, was Elisa. The woman who had shown me such kindness at my grandmother's estate. Next to her walked a beautiful little girl wearing a familiar-looking dark blue dress. She did not look my way or acknowledge me whatsoever. But she did hold her daughter's hand tightly, not letting go. They both laughed. There was no recollection of the world that she and her daughter had been saved from, but she still wore a veil of familiarity somewhere deep in her mind.

Somehow, she knew that pain. Somehow, she knew that loss, and therefore, she was profoundly grateful for what she had, holding onto it tightly.

My wool socks felt warm against the cold wood floor that creaked under my soft steps. I could smell breakfast, I could hear my mother humming a gentle melody, and I could hear my father laughing loudly as he read the morning paper, always looking at the cartoons first. I walked into the kitchen; there they were. My parents. Alive and well, as if nothing had happened. The entire world had been resurrected and the air was clearer than it had ever been. I couldn't help but just stare blankly at them. I was in awe of the love that was radiating from this dream-like moment. A warmth that I had never expected to feel again. I smiled while trying to hold back my tears of joy.

"Are you alright, sweetheart?' asked my mother.

"Yes. Yes, I'm fine, mother."

She smiled at me with a strange expression tucked behind the curves of her lips. The kind of look a mother gives you when they are willing to accept your reply but are obviously suspicious of its origin. She knew that something was hiding behind these tearful eyes.

"Okay. Well, come and have some breakfast. Just some simple eggs, with a side of blueberries for my little kingfisher," she teased.

As I sat down, I looked at the chair across from me and remembered a dinner party we had a couple of years ago. My father had invited over a man named Louis. A man that I knew from my other past, who had sheltered me at the start of my journey and found me amongst the rubble and death. Turns out, he was a friend of my father, who had been invited over for supper. He got along marvelously with my mother and me, and this was the first of many dinners that he would join us for. He even came over on holidays, bringing gifts and delicious food. He never had any children of his own, so he had taken a liking to me, even teaching me to paint. A promise that he had made to me in another lifetime. Because even within this new future, Louis was still helping to guide my step.

My father finished his breakfast and got ready to go to work for the day. As was his tradition, he kissed my mother and then ruffled my hair a little bit as he walked past, laughing the whole while.

"Off I go, ladies. I will see you both tonight," he announced as he made his way to the front door.

I could hear the front door open, letting in the bustling sounds of a city that was alive and full of movements. Children playing, businessmen marching, birds chirping, and carriages being pulled. A moment of beautiful chaos before the door would shut and my mother and I would be left in silence. But the door did not shut. Instead, we both heard my father's voice echo from down the hall.

"Darling… um… we have a visitor," he said.

My mother looked confused as she stood up from the table and made her way into the other room. Her shuffled steps suddenly halted as she made her way down the hall, and I could hear her gasp as if the breath had been sucked from her lungs.

"Mother?!" she exclaimed.

I jumped up from the table and ran into the hallway, finding my grandmother standing at our doorway, her eyes immediately catching mine, before darting back to my mother. She looked stern and focused, like she did in that picture I had found from my mother's youth. I froze. I did not know what to say. Why was she here? I remembered that in this life, I had never met her, even though in my other life we had gone on a marvelous journey together. Surely, she had no memory of this. No one besides me had any memory of the horrors that our world had endured. As such, she would not be the same woman whom I had met. That caring nature would never have been birthed had it not been for the rift.

"Mother, what are you doing here?"

My grandmother was silent at first. Looking as if she were about to scold or curse at any moment. She looked at my father and then at my mother, not a word let loose. Then, without warning, she grabbed my mother and hugged her. My mother was quite taken aback by this and was not sure how to react. She did not have any memories of being hugged by her mother during her youth. My grandmother started to cry as my mother finally returned her embrace.

She then stopped hugging my mother and took a moment to dry her eyes before looking directly at my father, who was in shock at what was happening. My grandmother then smiled at him.

"Thank you for taking such good care of my little girl," she said, before embracing my father and starting to cry all over again.

   My grandmother did not say anything to me, not even acknowledging my presence. She just asked my mother if there was somewhere private where the three of them could talk. They moved into the living room.

"Nicolette, darling, I know you are excited to meet your grandmother, but could you please give us a few moments to talk? Go and play or something?"

   I nodded while staring past my mother, hoping to once again lock eyes with my grandmother, who had yet to say a word to me. They then proceeded to go into the living room and sit down. I tried my best to hear everything that was being said in that room. But from behind walls, hiding in corners, it was hard to make much out. It sounded like a fair amount of crying, laughing, talking, and on occasion yelling. This went on for around an hour. Finally, my mother and father emerged from the living room, smiling, and drying their tears, before my father, who was running quite late, left for work.

"Nicolette?!" my mother yelled.

"Yes?" I replied, appearing from just beyond the other side of the living room wall.

"Your grandmother has requested to meet you and speak to you alone."

"Okay," I replied nervously.

I made my way into the living room, my grandmother sitting in a chair and facing away from me. This moment reminded me of the first time that we had met. Except we were no longer in a library, surrounded by literary adventures, with our faces lit up by the soft glow of a fire.

"Don't be shy, Nicolette. Come and sit next to me," she said.

I sat down on the floor next to her. It felt wonderful to be in her presence once again, basking in her mighty shadow. Even though she was not the same woman that I had known, I just hoped that whatever had fueled her to arrive here and shower my mother and father with her embrace, was enough to make her a good person. The person that I had known.

She glanced down at me and then looked back towards the living room entrance, making sure we were truly alone before a subtle smile crept across her face. I studied her eyes. And as I did so, I noticed something… familiar.

"I woke up yesterday morning, Nicolette," she started. "And I immediately realized that I had to come here. I had no rhyme or reason for doing so. After all, I've spent countless years being angry and bitter at your mother and the life that she'd made for herself. But I had a feeling that would not subside no matter how much I tried to ignore it. Then, as Mr. Oswald steered the carriage towards the city, under night skies and eager mornings, I started to remember things. Things that I had not lived, but nevertheless knew. Things that softened my heart and held my breath. These memories guided my step and led me to this house and its front door. And there I waited, scared to knock, tempted to run, until your father opened that door, and forced my hand."

My grandmother went silent as a single tear rolled down her cheek.

"You did it, Nicolette. You saved the world. And better yet… I remember everything!"

I smiled wide and jumped from the ground, embracing my grandmother, and crying tears of joy. She was as I had known her, and what's more, she was here.

"But how do you remember?" I asked. "The last time I saw you, you were trapped behind the garden walls."

"I remember you disappearing into the darkness, leaving me in worry and loss, scared of what was to become of you. Then, suddenly, like magic, I woke up back in my bedroom. That life that I had been leading had ended, and I was left in the comfort of a miserable past and a bright future. I cannot explain why it happened, only that it did."

I couldn't believe it. My grandmother and I were the only ones who actually remembered the great war. We were the only ones who knew of the horror and beauty that the rift had brought into this world. We were now the guardians of the biggest secret that had ever been.

"So, what do we do now?" I asked.

"We live. We live and we smile, and we laugh loudly and frequently," she replied.

At that exact moment, I heard a familiar grumble and cough come from just outside the house, accompanied by the stench of tobacco.

"Smile and laugh? But isn't Mr. Oswald as grumpy as ever?" I asked with a giggle.

My grandmother laughed.

"Well... *most* of us will smile and laugh," she said with a little wink.

That night, we all sat down to dinner. My mother, father, grandmother, and even mean old Mr. Oswald. We started anew. A second chance one only finds within the dreams of fools. After dinner, I laid down in bed, and my mother and grandmother read me a story, switching off reading every other page. One of my favorites.

And as their words started to fade, and my eyes grew heavy, I couldn't help but wonder something. What if every time we wake up and greet the day with hope in our step, is a second chance that we don't know about? What if someone else has found a dying star and turned back the clock? Chance after chance, and a mysterious feeling of hope erupting from our very being. Maybe every day, when we can find hope, is a fresh start and a second chance. A chance to find hope, love, and forgiveness. To take those first steps out of bed and realize the miracle of being alive.

I drifted off to sleep as my dreams filled with other worlds and second chances. The last words echoing within my mind:

> *"She thought to herself, 'This is right now.' She was happy that the little cottage, and her ma and pa, and the warm fire, and the music, were right now. They could not be forgotten, she thought, because now is now. It can never really be a long time ago."*

The End

Thank you for reading and coming along on this journey!

If you enjoyed this story, please check out these other works by Nathan Harms.

Until next time, dear reader.

Interra

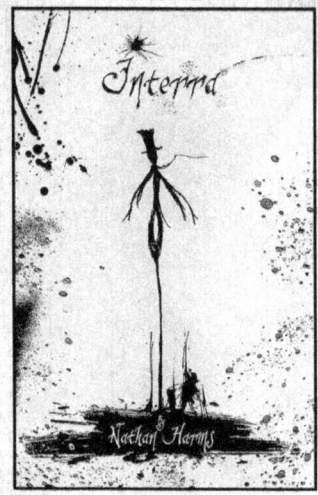

Paperback:979-8-7216-7342-9
Hardcover:979-8-5040-4812-3

I Was a Forest

Paperback:979-8-4259-5967-6
Hardcover:979-8-4259-6474-8

Good Bird

Paperback:979-8-8315-9860-5
Hardcover:979-8-8315-9922-0

The Theory of Thought

Paperback:979-8-8488-7328-3
Hardcover:979-8-8488-7353-5

Petrichor

Paperback:979-8-3729-8965-8
Hardcover:979-8-3729-8981-8

The Viridian Rift

Paperback:979-8-8599-7701-7
Hardcover:979-8-8599-7712-3

Own The Full Collection in
'One Foot in Front of the Other'
The Collected Works of Nathan Harms Vol. 1

Paperback:979-8-8600-4202-5

And keep up to date with future projects by visiting us at
HarmsPublications.com

Made in the USA
Middletown, DE
03 November 2024